The Rebel Christian Publishing

ISBN: 9781957290287 (eBook)
Print: 9781957290294

This is a work of fiction. Any references to historical events, real people, or real places are used fictitiously. Names, characters, and places are products of the author's imagination. Inclusion of or reference to any Christian elements or themes are used in a fictitious manner and are not meant to be perceived or interpreted as an act of disrespect against such a wonderful and beautiful belief system.

Cover image provided by Envato Elements
Cover designed by Valicity Elaine

The Rebel Christian Publishing LLC
350 Northern Blvd STE 324 - 1390
Albany, NY 12204-1000

Visit us: http://www.therebelchristian.com/
Email us: rebel@therebelchristian.com

Contents

* * *WARNING* * *
Author's Note

Hello! If you've read my romantic suspense trilogy, _Withered Rose_, then you already know what I'm about to say. But if you're new here, welcome!

The first thing you need to know about my books is that they are works of Christian fiction. I shamelessly believe the Bible is 100 percent true. I believe Christ is the Messiah—my Savior—and I believe the Holy Spirit is my guidance and God is my Father.

Due to my beliefs, I have strived to write this novel in a manner fit for Christian audiences, but I will never make the claim that this story—or any of my stories—are 'Clean and Wholesome.' The truth is, real life is not clean and wholesome, otherwise, we wouldn't need a Savior. I write characters that are flawed— perfectly imperfect—and I enjoy portraying them in raw honesty. The goal is to demonstrate that God can save, use, and love even the worst of us.

There is no foul language in this book. There are no graphic scenes of sex. There is no graphic violence. However, this book is intended for mature Christian audiences. Topics such as manipulation, imprisonment, gang activity, assault, and psychological illness are explored in this story.

If you are a sensitive reader, I urge you to proceed with caution or perhaps enjoy one of my other novels instead.

Fractured Diamond is a standalone spinoff novel taking place in the crime ridden world of the *Withered Rose trilogy*. Some characters from the predecessor series make an appearance in this book but the plot is unrelated and can be enjoyed without reading the original trilogy.

Thank you, please enjoy.

Fractured Diamond

By Valicity Elaine

A Rebel Christian Publishing Book

1

A job interview is probably one of the most stressful things to dress for. Should I wear my little black dress? Make it more casual by adding my favorite blazer so no one thinks I'm trying to seduce my way into a contract. What about stockings? No. It's mid-July, the only stockings I'll suffer through in this heat are fishnets and we can both agree that's not the best thing to wear in an interview.

So … No stockings. That leaves shoes. The little buggers.

Heels? Sure, but not more than four inches—actually, cut it down to three or I'll definitely get accused of the seduction act. But my only pair of heels lower than four inches is a pathetic pair of brown oxfords my mother gave me two birthdays ago. One of them is scuffed on the toe.

Fine, four-inch heels but only if they're black.

Accessories.

Simple studs with my matching silver chain and cross pendant. I'll keep the hair loose today—yes, it's a mop of tight curls that most will find 'unprofessional' or 'inappropriate' for the workplace, but there are perks to being the owner of said workplace, right?

Today's interview is not about me landing a job at all, it's about me hiring someone to fill a job—though it's still important my scheduled candidate likes me *somewhat*.

I sigh as I look at my reflection. At least he's getting paid for all this. If all goes well, I'll be out of fifty-two thousand dollars—half up front.

I can't be *too* upset about the price. I am asking for six months of personal security 24/7. That's half a year's wages. All of that just to follow me around all day. For some reason, I feel sorry for the guy. Admittedly, I can be a pain. But then I remember fifty-two thousand (half up front) and my pity goes out the window. I mean, my business is successful, but this is a stretch even for me.

You'd think selling diamonds would make me an instant millionaire, right?

We *did* bring in 2.3 million in sales last year, but we also accrued 2.1 million in costs. I barely had enough to pay my one employee, and she's only parttime.

Gem Jewelers is barely staying afloat.

With those numbers, I really shouldn't be shedding cash on personal security, but this isn't something I'm doing for fun, believe me. The last thing I want is some beefcake following me everywhere I go all day long. But after what happened eight weeks ago, I'm not taking my chances anymore. My back still aches at the memory, but it's the nightmares that are most painful.

At night, it all comes back to me. The rain on my lashes, trying to blink away the water as I punched the alarm for the store. The slow crawl of fear that'd slithered up my spine when I'd turned around and saw the hooded man. A flash of silver. My hands going up. A scream. My heels clacking on the sidewalk as I'd tried to run—his footsteps right behind me. Getting closer. And then a shred of pain tearing into me from behind.

I'd been stabbed in the back. Slashed up like confetti.

The shocking thing about it is I hadn't been robbed. The jerk just stabbed me and ran. I suppose he'd intended to kill me or send a message but to whom and what for hasn't been figured out yet.

To be honest, I really don't care. I'm just happy to be alive, especially since that was the second time I'd faced a terrible assault.

The first time happened when I was eighteen. I remember that night from years ago as clearly as the assault two months in the past. Another thug with a knife, the only difference that time being the presence of my boyfriend. What help he offered. I still had a knife held to my throat; I still endured pain that's left me with scars I wear today. I hadn't expected my boyfriend to go all Batman on the guy and break his neck, but I also hadn't expected him to do *nothing*.

To just stand and watch.

My friends and family have always believed he played a part in it all. Considering the fact that he disappeared afterward. I've always believed it too.

I subconsciously rub the cross dangling around my neck as my intercom buzzes. Lyla, my lovely assistant, speaks in a chipper voice, "Your one o'clock is here, Ms. Gem."

I tap the button. "Send him in."

I turn around and face the window of my office as I wait for the sound of the door to chime open. My eyes are closed, and my chest is filled with air. I'm holding my breath, trying not to freak out. I really shouldn't have gone down memory lane right before my first interview. I feel like I'm about to have a panic attack right in the middle of my own office.

My hand twitches as I fight the urge to reach into my desk drawer and grab my meds—something I was given for anxiety. I haven't been taking them. I don't want them. *All I need is to calm down*, I tell myself, and like a genie from a bottle, the smooth voice across the room grants my internal wish.

"You're okay."

It isn't a question—it's a statement. A firm belief that I am indeed fine and that this brief moment of panic will pass.

I shudder, slightly embarrassed that my client walked in on me freaking out, but the embarrassment doesn't last long. When I turn around, it's replaced by a violent jolt of shock.

I recognize the man before me right away. How could I not? It doesn't matter that it's been six years, I'd know this man after six *centuries*.

My one o'clock interview is none other than Robert Ackard.

On my desk is his file, which I quickly glance at as he

smirks at me from across the room. His name is right there, in bold letters. But I hadn't looked at his file—Lyla had done all the vetting, and I'd trusted that she wouldn't let my ex-boyfriend slip through the pile.

"Rob?" my voice is but a whisper and I hate it because the sound of his name on my lips makes me weak in the knees all of a sudden.

Robert Ackard.

He'd gone by *Bobby* when we were in school. Of course he went by Bobby... All the girls had loved his nickname, like he was some bad boy heartthrob from cable TV. He *was* a bad boy heartthrob, and he had the looks to be on TV back then, but still... He shouldn't look that way anymore. The fact that he does sends my heart doing cartwheels through my chest.

I will *not* do him the liberty of a detailed description. Just know that his blue eyes are still sharp enough to pierce my heart, and his smile is as dangerous as it's ever been.

The corner of his mouth turns up the slightest bit, it's a look Bobby mastered in high school. Something that teeters between a charming smile and a teasing grin. I hate that look. Because I used to love it. But things are different now. I'm not a starry-eyed teenager madly in love with her high school crush, I'm a businesswoman who was literally stabbed in the back— twice now.

"What on earth are you doing here?" I snap—and just like that, all my anxiety is magically gone. Told you I didn't need the meds.

Bobby takes a step forward and I launch like a cat. *"Don't*

5

come any closer!" My hands fly up like I'm ready to claw his eyes out if he takes another step, but there is no shock on his face, no surprise in my sudden outburst. That's because he knows it isn't so sudden.

There's a reason I hate my old boyfriend of two years. There's a reason the sight of my high school sweetheart brings burning tears to my eyes. Bobby's presence is shocking enough to bring attention to his charm and his handsome appearance, but riding on the coattails of his pretty smile is the reminder of our past. This isn't a nice gentleman returning for a shot at love, this is my boyfriend who watched me get stabbed, and then ran away afterward—but it gets better.

Bobby didn't run while the guy still had the knife in his hand. It was weeks later, after I was released from the hospital and had finally worked up the strength to attend high school graduation. My family threw me a party, in celebration of my achievement and in joy of my recovery. Bobby had attended, had told me how much he loved me, how sorry he was that he'd gotten spooked by the whole assault.

We made love for the first time that night, each passionate kiss melting away the pain of the nightmare I'd lived through. Bobby had swept me off my feet. He'd made my world whole again.

And then he left.

Vanished like he'd never existed—all on the night that I'd given him my heart, mind, and body. He'd given his thanks via sticky note left by the bed.

I grit my teeth at the memory, at the thought of my younger

self reading his stupid little goodbye note with my hand balling fists into the sheets. Pathetically, I still have that stupid sticky note. I didn't have it in me to throw it away, despite all the raw hatred, anger, and bitterness I'd suffered from that whole situation. Two years of my life with him, and it ended in one night without a single word in explanation.

Maybe that's why I kept the note. To remind myself that liars, scumbags, and snakes are not the shady looking ones with missing teeth and a lazy eye. No, the snake in my life is a charming blonde in a pressed suit.

Bobby stuffs his hands into his pockets. "All right. I'll stay right here, Bri."

"*Brianna*," I correct him sharply. He doesn't get to use my nickname anymore. "Actually, it's Ms. Gem to everyone who isn't a friend."

Bobby nods. "Fair enough, *Ms. Gem*."

"What are you doing here?" I snap.

"The interview."

"You knew Gem Jewelers was my business when you filled out the application."

"Actually, I didn't fill out the application." He shrugs his shoulders, it's such a smooth, fluid motion, I actually watch the corners of his suit jacket crinkle and then settle on his lean frame.

His voice draws me back.

"The company I work for saw the bulletin and applied in my place."

"But you accepted the interview."

"I did."

"Even though you knew it was my business."

"Yes."

"Why?"

"Because I knew there was no other way I could get you to speak to me."

"You had *six years* to speak to me," I hiss, and I hope to God I sound like a pit viper because that's what I feel like right now. My words drip from my mouth, each one meant to sting like venom. "What happened in all that time?" I scoff. "Couldn't find another sticky note?"

There is a grin on his face, but I see the flicker of emotion that passes through his eyes before he says, "The fact that you're still angry about our breakup says a lot."

I burn. "I'm not just angry about losing my high school boyfriend. I'm angry about everything else! And the fact that you can stand here and sum things up to bitter heartbreak proves just how disgusting you truly are."

"Brianna, I'm just trying to lighten the air."

Spit flies from my mouth as I practically scream, "I got *stabbed* and you want to lighten the air?"

On cue, the intercom buzzes and Lyla's pleasant voice comes over the little speaker. "Everything okay, Ms. Gem?"

I clear my throat and take three deep breaths, nostrils flaring. "Yes, everything is good."

Lyla buzzes back right away. "Your next appointment will be here in ten minutes."

"Thank you, Lyla."

8

I don't have another appointment today; Bobby is my only one. But Lyla knows this already—her little heads-up was her way of giving me a chance to politely end things here and now with Bobby.

I glare at him, not caring that there are tears welling in my eyes.

"Get out," I say. It comes out in a whisper; that's all I can produce right now. When he doesn't move, I say it again. *"Get. Out."* There's a whimper woven into the words, my voice cracking with emotion.

Bobby catches it.

He swallows hard and stares at the floor before he says softly, "I'm willing to do the job for half of what you're offering."

My breath hitches. He can't be serious. Not only would it be a huge relief for my finances, but it would also be a burden lifted from this entire process. I wasn't lying when I said Bobby was my only interview today. He's been my only interview all week—probably because I'm not offering enough money.

You can find cheap security on Craig's List if you want, but I'm not looking to hire the fat guy with pit stains who guards the sliding doors of the Walmart Supercenter. I need a qualified guard who'll take a bullet for me.

After everything that's happened between us, I won't make the assumption that Bobby is willing to take a bullet for a girl he left six years ago, but right now he's the only one even willing to apply. And now he's saying he'll take the job for half the pay.

A very tired sigh blows from my lips as I lean over and grip the sides of my desk. This can't be happening right now. Bobby Ackard cannot be in my office. My business cannot be doing this poorly two years into the industry. I cannot be in a corner, forced to choose between no security or being guarded by my scumbag ex-boyfriend.

Bobby fishes something from his pocket, when his business card slides onto the desk, into my line of sight, I snap my head up at him. "I told you not to come any closer."

"You seem calm enough to approach."

"I don't want your business card."

He smirks.

I resist the urge to spit at him.

"My business number is on the bottom. My personal number is on the back."

"I don't care."

His grin widens, and he winks. "Yes, you do."

2

Celery crunches between my mother's teeth as she enjoys her charcuterie board. The only reason I agreed to have lunch with her is because I truly had nothing else to do. I'd cleared my schedule for the day, anticipating a slew of candidates to interview. With Bobby being my one and only, and having kicked him out of my office in less than three minutes, I'm officially free for the day.

I could have gotten some other work done. Taken inventory, polished some of the display jewelry, checked the analytics for our website. But after bumping into my ex-boyfriend like that, I'm not in the mood for anything.

Well... I stare at the bottle of wine the waiter left at our table. There is one thing I'm in the mood for, but I wouldn't dare have a glass in front of my mother. Not *because* she's my mother, but because she's my overbearing, headache inducing, Christian mother. Don't get me wrong—I love Jesus too, but my dear mom is the type of Christian who loves reminding you of everything you have ever done wrong in your entire life. And she loves finishing my pretty rap sheet with a reminder that we're all forgiven.

"God remembers our sins no more," she says, patting my hand.

Apparently, He's the only one who doesn't remember. And if, by chance, He ever needed a reminder of my wrongdoing, I know a woman who'd be happy to list every *single* sin I've ever committed.

I force a smile and pluck my eyeballs from the wine bottle to return my gaze to my mother. She's still patting my hand, waiting for a response to *whatevertheheck* she was saying before I started daydreaming about guzzling the deep red that's been calling my name since Bobby walked out my office.

Gosh ... I can still smell his cologne, like he stuffed a cotton swab of it up my flared nostrils. Smooth and rich, like the *fragrance* of pure gold. That's what he was, a thicc bar of gold walking around my office. Yes ... a *THICC* one—not a thick one.

But despite the refined nature of his scent, nothing else about Bobby Ackard has changed. He's still got that rugged look to him, dirty blonde hair with an equally dirty smirk, strong shoulders that broadened with age. He's all man now, not the thin kid with the crooked grin from trigonometry class. Even his attitude hasn't changed, I could tell that much just from looking at the arrogant gleam in his eye.

Bobby has always been trouble. He was that scholarship kid who didn't belong at Manhattan Academic Prep, which is exactly why I lost my mind over him. And exactly why my parents never approved of him.

He'd come from the wrong side of the tracks. Rumor had it his family had ties with the mafia, which made my heart go wild. I was a sheltered Christian girl, and he was a mafia rebel at some prissy prep school in New York City. We had no business getting involved, but I was curious, and he was interested. My quiet family-life intrigued him, his dangerous spontaneity had cast a spell on me.

But as fiery and mystifying *I* thought Bobby was, my parents had a completely different idea of him. My very vocal father had called him 'trailer trash' and had even gone as far as speaking to my principal about having Bobby's scholarship revoked. To my pleasure—and Daddy's horror—the school board rejected his request.

As much as my parents hated Bobby and his rumored gang affiliation, the truth was that neither of us had broken any rules by dating. Administration wasn't going to take away his only means of getting an education just because the mighty Colonel Gem said so.

Yes … my father's name is actually Colonel. No, he is not an *actual* colonel. It's my dumb grandfather's idea of giving him a strong name at birth—a *man's* name, as he'd always reminded us at longsuffering Christmas dinners, gumming his mashed potatoes while he spoke.

I come from a long line of jewelers. Some great grandpappy I never met started Gem Co. before my other grandpappies were born, and here I am. Got my own storefront that's barely hanging on by a thread. Meanwhile,

13

Daddy's thirteen jewelry stores are flourishing, and my older brother's two stores are steady. I am *that* child. Not quite disappointing but also not worth a Christmas card whenever I spend holidays away from the family.

Oh well, at least I can afford my own place. God knows I suffered enough growing up in that household; having to live with my parents as an adult would drive me nuts.

I blow a sigh as my mother prattles on about a new collection of chocolate diamonds my brother Greyson got his hands on recently. I'm not listening and I'm *this* close to reaching for that wine bottle just to change the subject and get yelled at, but before I can make the mistake of the week, the waiter strolls over and introduces a very late guest.

My cousin Verna. She beams at us as she plops into a seat, ignoring Mama's scowl and greeting me with an air kiss.

I love my cousin Verna. Not because she's the only supportive family member I have, I love her because she finds herself at the end of my mother's scrutiny as often as I do. Despite the fact that Verna is her brother's daughter, Mama doesn't like my sweet cousin. Really, she doesn't like that entire side of the family. Says they're too 'blue collar' which is her fancy way of saying they're poor.

That's insulting for multiple reasons, but I'll go over the two that frustrate me the most.

First of all, Verna is from *her* side of the family. My mother did not grow up with the bank account she has now. She was raised by a humble marine and his sweet Bible study teacher of a wife. Somehow, Mom met The Colonel and turned into this

14

celery sucking woman before me now.

Second reason I get irritated at her irritation toward Verna is the fact that Verna isn't actually poor—despite what my mother would like to believe. Verna's father, my Uncle Jerome Lee, is the Police Commissioner of NYPD and his wife is a fairly successful lawyer. They're not millionaires, but they sure aren't poor. And even if they were, no one deserves my mother's scrutiny. At least not because of their financial status.

Thankfully, Verna takes the scowls and snide insults in stride. With all the elegance of a princess, she sits beside me and prepares herself a fancy little plate of cheese, specialty crackers, and caviar from the charcuterie display. When she's poured herself a glass of sparkling lemonade, she flips her hair over her shoulder and smiles at my mother.

"Afternoon, Aunt Shelly."

Mom smiles back, and it looks like glass cracking. "Afternoon."

I figure this would be a lovely time to excuse myself and leave these two lovebirds alone, but I don't want to punish Verna—plus, my phone beeps with an alert and I suddenly remember it's time for my pills.

Apparently, my mother remembers too. She raises an eyebrow at me as I dig through my purse. "Still on the meds?"

I resist the urge to sigh. Yet another sinful thing my mother hates about me. I'm a Christian who takes anxiety meds. It's taboo in the religious community, but I can't deny the illness that's clearly plaguing me. Ever since the most recent assault, I haven't been able to stop my hands from shaking without the

15

meds. I hate taking them as much as my mother does—and I try to avoid them whenever possible—but after encountering Bobby and then being subject to Mama's scrutiny for two hours, I'm fed up.

At this point, it's either the wine or the meds. Mom can take her pick.

She gives me a little harrumph as I count each pill. One for anxiety, one for the nausea the anxiety pill causes, an anti-depressant to keep my spirits high on crap days like today, and a pill that helps prevent ulcers because—naturally—taking a handful of pills can sometimes cause pain inducing pus balls to eat away at your insides.

I ignore my mom as I toss back the pills and reach for my water, thankful for the reassuring smile Verna gives me in the silence that follows. She's the only one who never judged me or blamed me for what happened. Even when I blamed myself.

I shouldn't have been alone at night. I should've locked up much earlier. I should've been watching my back.

Or maybe some guy shouldn't have slashed you up with a knife— how about that?

That's what Verna told me when I'd broken down in tears a few weeks ago, suffering my first ever anxiety attack. Lungs restricting, vision blurring, it was the worst experience of my life. But sweet Verna had been there for me, and she's still here now.

Meanwhile, everyone else in my life only felt the need to point out everything I did wrong in that scenario. And now I'm being scrutinized for something as small as a pill I don't even

16

want to take.

"When I was your age, we didn't believe in all those pills," Mom says with a huff.

I ignore her, though it takes effort.

"I'm praying for you," sweet Verna says. "You'll be off the meds in no time."

I nod. "Thank you, Verna."

She pats my hand. "I'll send you some Scriptures to say before bed every night."

"Right after she tosses back another handful of drugs, right?" Mom inserts.

Would it kill her to just keep quiet...

I almost scream at her, but my phone beeps again and I snatch it up just to have something else to focus on. It's a message from Greyson, a picture of his new display. A beautiful arrangement of chocolate diamonds sits in the middle of his gorgeous store, winking in the light.

I deflate.

Greyson is a cool brother, except when he's competing with me—which is all the time. It started when I opened Gem Jewelers; somehow, he saw me as a threat and has tried his hardest to undermine or insult me at every turn.

I'm not a sore loser, I can admit that my successful brother, who's eight years my senior, is better at selling jewelry than I am. But I can also admit that the little reminders of his greatness he likes to leave around can sometimes get under my skin.

The only time Greyson was ever genuinely nice to me was

17

right after the last assault. He had blamed me, saying I shouldn't have ever closed the shop alone, but he'd also taken the reins and ran the store while I was recovering. He added an upgraded security system with surveillance all on his own dime, and when it was time for him to leave, he gave me a choice—sell him the storefront or hire security.

Obviously, I chose the latter, though I'll admit … I should have sold the thing.

I'm in over my head, but I'm too stubborn to give up. I want to prove my brother wrong, that I'm not the loser sibling. I want to prove my father wrong, that I am worthy of the legacy I've been born into. And I want to prove myself wrong, that I can recover from everything I've experienced.

Bobby messed me up. My own struggles with the business messed me up. The assault nearly killed me. And now all the pills and the constant judgment. But I won't let it take me down. I'm better than this. Stronger than this.

Tough as diamonds—that's what The Colonel likes to say. Not about me, but still. I'll prove I can be that tough. One day.

My lips part as the meds do their work. I feel everything kick in at once. My anger toward my family melts away. The nervous jitters subside. The bout of nausea that'd threatened to return the caviar I'd eaten ebbs away.

I am calm.

Mom notices the shift in my demeanor and sucks her teeth. "This is why I don't trust those pills. They change your brain."

"I know, Mom," I say calmly.

"Devil's work," she grumbles, reaching for another celery

stick.

Whelp, this is as good as our lunch is going to get.

I stand and reach for my purse, squeezing Verna's shoulder before I head out. "Sorry I can't stay any longer."

She smiles up at me. "Take care of yourself, Bri."

At home, I sit on the edge of my bed and stare at the screen of my phone. The picture of Greyson's chocolate diamonds burns into my eyes, filling me with a jealousy I don't need. My store has never had a special display, not even for Valentine's Day. We've never been able to afford the diamonds. Most of the jewelry we sell comes from old collections my brother was generous enough to gift me when my doors first opened. Since then, we've only had the funds to buy cheaper versions of what we've always had. Nothing new. Nothing more.

I want some specialty diamonds. I want a full display of glittering jewels lighting up the middle of my store. I want a fat ruby or a sapphire the size of an egg.

I fall back onto my bed, staring at the ceiling, thinking of the last time I'd worked up the courage to ask my parents for a loan so I could buy a holiday collection. My mother's snippy remarks weren't even needed—my father cut me down all on his own. Called me a spoiled princess who needed to learn the value of hard work.

Spoiled princess.

It's something Bobby had called me while we were

together, though he'd always said it in a joking sort of way, full of flirtation and kindness. His eyes smiling as much as his mouth, crinkled in the corners.

"You're such a spoiled princess, Bri," he would always say. And as soon as I'd turn to give him attitude about it, he'd pull me into his arms and silence me with a kiss, laughing against my lips. "But you're *my* princess. You hear? You're mine, Bri."

And I was. Until I wasn't.

Pathetically, I slide off my bed and walk to the corner table. Inside the bottom drawer, stuck to the last page of my old diary, is the sticky note Bobby left me all those years ago. Despite the tears blurring my vision, I can make out every word written in his harried penmanship. Like he'd quickly scribbled down a grocery list before heading out to the market.

It's been fun, Princess.

I choke on a sob.

I know my day has gone to crap when I pull out the good ol' sticky note, but it's been a long time since the note has made me cry. Maybe it's all the emotion from seeing him today. Maybe it's the built-up frustration of having lunch with my mom. Maybe it's the gnawing jealousy of seeing Greyson's display.

Whatever the case, I just want the ache in my chest to end.

Wiping at my tears, I toss the diary onto my bed and march to my kitchen. There's a half-empty bottle of wine I swore I wouldn't finish, but I grab it now and march back to my room fully determined to break that promise and drink away the guilt that'll follow.

But I never do.

I lie on the bed again, staring at the sticky note to my right and the chocolate diamonds on my left. I can't decide which is worse to look at right now, but I stay there for hours, rooted in place. Anchored by pain.

Only the beep of my phone stirs me back to life. I know what the alert is even before swiping it away; it's pill time yet again. But just as I roll over to search for my purse, my phone beeps once more and I glance back to find a text from Verna.

Here are the Scriptures I promised!

She lists only three and I read them all, muttering them aloud to myself. Then I glance around my room like I'm a stranger who just woke up here. The half-empty bottle of wine still decorates my bedside table. My meds are somewhere in my purse, waiting for me to answer their call.

If I want to prove anything to anyone, I've got to start with myself.

With resolve I didn't know I had, I pour the wine down the sink and kick my purse across the room. I'm stronger than this. Even though my hands still shake as I climb into bed, even though my heart still aches as I tuck my old diary away, I know whatever tears I've shed today will turn to joy by the morning. At least, that's the prayer I mumble before I drift off into a dreamless sleep.

3

The store smells like vanilla and sugar when I walk in this morning. It immediately puts me in a good mood. The lights automatically flash on as I stroll toward the back where my little office is located, along with a tiny alcove for Lyla to huddle at her desk—right in front of our mostly empty vault that's poorly hidden behind a satin black curtain that cuts off the back of the room. I have a mini fridge and a coatrack on the other side of the curtain, along with a microwave that needs cleaning, and a single stall bathroom.

We aren't Tiffany's by a long shot, but it could be worse.

In my office, I dump my purse and tap my stopwatch as it chimes a reminder for me to take my meds. The day is just getting started, I don't feel that I need any pills first thing in the morning, so I silence the alarm and grab a seltzer water from the mini fridge.

As I head back to my office, seltzer water in hand, I nearly scream when I see Lyla pushing open the backdoor. She jumps when she spots me and both of us gape at each other.

"You nearly gave me a heart attack!" I clutch my chest dramatically.

She gasps. "I'm sorry, Ms. Gem! I came in early to get you prepped for your interviews."

I roll my eyes, thinking of my last one. "Do we have any biters?"

"Not yet—"

"Then how are you going to prep me?"

"Well, the one from yesterday called again—"

I start shaking my head. "The answer is no."

"No?"

"We're not hiring him."

"But he's perfect."

I grind my teeth together. "I said no, Lyla."

She drops her things onto her desk and blinks at me. Lyla is only nineteen, too young and naïve to realize she should be making double what I'm paying her, but she's a good girl. She knows how to handle all my mood swings and has learned when to wisely keep quiet, like right now.

Ignoring her questioning eyes, I give her a nod and turn toward my office. "I'll be out in time to open."

Poor Lyla spends her morning typing away on her computer. I keep my door shut and ignore her sighs as I try to concentrate on my emails. No matter how many times I refresh my inbox, nothing new pops up. The only candidate we've got is still Bobby. Even though he's offering to work for half the price, I'm not convinced the deal will be worth it. The business could seriously benefit from hiring him, but I'd planned to spend 52k from the start, we won't fall behind if we decide to hire someone else. But we don't even have the option to hire someone else right now.

No one wants to work for us.

I sigh and close my laptop, it's just before nine in the morning. Time to open the store.

Lyla is polishing a set of diamond studded earrings when I enter the main area of the shop. "Ready for the day?" she asks in a chipper voice.

I nod. "I'll work the front today."

"Are you sure? I don't mind—"

"I'm positive," I say quickly. I don't mean to snap at her, but I can't be locked up in my office right now. I'll just drive myself insane with thoughts I shouldn't think. I need to keep busy or else I might cave, call Bobby, and hire him on the spot. His card is still on my desk, hidden beneath a bunch of junk mail. I should have thrown it out when he first gave it to me, but I left the office right after he did.

Lyla touches my shoulder. "I'll be in the back if you need anything."

"Thanks, Lyla."

The morning flies by. We get a few customers who try on jewelry and even place a few orders. When the store filters out, I keep myself occupied by polishing the display shelves and taking calls on the phone at the front desk. And then, just as I'm starting to feel confident, Lyla pops her head in to crush my hopes.

"A client called," she says nervously.

My face splits into a smile but it quickly withers at the sight of her anxious face. "Who was it?" I ask cautiously.

She clears her throat. "Robert Ackard."

I frown. "I told you—"

"I know!" she quickly inserts. "But he called to inquire about the status of his application and—"

"And what did you tell him?"

"I told him that we still haven't decided."

"We *have* decided," I grunt.

"Ms. Gem, I think he's an excellent candidate."

I know she does. *Of course* she does. But that's only because she *doesn't* know who Robert Ackard really is—and I'm not about to explain that to her because it would put me in a really awkward position. I like Lyla, but I don't want to tell her about my crappy love life.

"If he calls again, block him," I say in a stern voice.

Lyla pouts. "Yes, ma'am."

"Actually," I turn toward my office, "I'll just end this now."

"What do you mean?"

"I'm going to call him and tell him we've hired someone else."

"But we haven't."

"I know that, Lyla." I roll my eyes and kick my office door shut behind me. I just want to be done with Bobby for good. Better to rip the bandage off now and get this over with. We still don't have any other candidates, but I'd rather forgo security altogether than work with him—even at half the price.

I find his stupid business card on my desk and grab my

phone; my hand shakes as I dial his personal number. The phone rings only once—and then I hang up.

What if this is what he wants? For me to get worked up enough to give him a call. He'd said the only reason he scheduled an interview was to talk to me. His words dance through my head again and the sound of his smooth timbre sends chills ghosting over my bare arms.

I knew this was the only way you'd ever speak to me.

Before I can think too deeply about what he'd said, my phone buzzes in my hand. It scares me so badly, I yelp and almost drop it on my desk. Then I almost throw it across the room when I recognize the number.

It's Bobby. He's calling me back.

I sigh.

"Hello?" I say, pressing the phone to my hear.

Bobby's voice is buttery, melting into my ear as he chuckles. "You called."

"Listen," I snap, "I don't know who you think you are, but you can't keep calling my business."

"I only called twice."

"Just leave me alone, Bobby."

"Look, I know this isn't the reunion you wanted—"

"Don't you *dare*," I hiss.

That actually shuts him up. I can hear his even breathing on the other end, calm and perfectly in control, unlike me who's panting so hard I'm sure my blood pressure is through the roof.

I take a deep breath. "Thank you for your interest in

working with Gem Jewelers, but upon further reflection, we have decided not to pursue a contract with you, Mr. Ackard."

I hear him exhale, and it's not the word he says next that startles me, it's the tone of his voice.

"Princess…"

Like he can somehow see through the phone, the lies, and my internal walls, Bobby cuts straight to my heart. I press the back of my hand to my mouth, so he doesn't hear me suck for breath. This isn't a panic attack at all, it's me desperately trying to hold back my tears. No one should have this much sway over my emotions. But here I am, a grown woman reduced to tears by a single word.

I burn with anger and shame and an embarrassing ache all at once. Yes, I *ache* for Bobby Ackard. Not a perverse desire to roll around my office floor with him, but a sad yearning for the intimacy we once shared. That he could look at me and know what I was thinking. That he could tell what I was feeling from the slightest exchange. That every part of me was an alarm to him, sending signals and clues of my innermost thoughts and secrets.

Bobby had learned everything about me. Had mastered me like I was a subject to be learned, a book to be read, a woman to be tamed. He had somehow learned the formula that'd alluded even me. And, apparently, he'd never forgotten.

His voice is in my ear, speaking gently. "Talk to me."

I shake my head, though I know he can't see it.

Not now. Not like this.

"I've got to go," I sniffle.

27

"Brianna—"

I hang up the phone and then I put it on silence and shove it in my desk drawer, so I won't hear if he calls back. And just to make sure I don't retrieve it and call him myself, I lock the desk drawer and leave the key with Lyla as I leave the office.

She gives me a queer look. "You're leaving your desk key with me?"

I nod. "Yes. Do not give it back until I ask for it. Understand?"

"Yes, ma'am."

"I'm going to work the front for the rest of the day. You can head home whenever you're ready."

"Thank you, Ms. Gem."

___oOo___

My phone is still in my desk drawer. Even though I know I need the darn thing, I never ask Lyla for the key because I know myself enough to admit that I'm a weakling. If I had my phone, I would have caved in and called Bobby during my lunch hour. Instead of suffering the shame of crawling back to my ex, I tell Lyla to take the key home with her.

I can check my email from my laptop and respond to anything important tomorrow. The only thing that trips me up is contacting my older brother. We're supposed to have dinner tonight, so I have to call him from the phone at the front desk to make sure we're still good. Aside from the awkward conversation where I have to explain why I'm not using my cell; I manage to survive the evening without my phone.

Honestly, I feel proud of myself as I sit with Greyson at his favorite restaurant. We're not the closest siblings by far, but when he's in a good mood, he forgets that we're supposed to hate and compete with each other for no real reason. That's when I realize how charming my brother can be, that he actually has a sense of humor behind his stylish glasses and curly hair weighed down by product. There's so much gel in his coils, I fear the flakes will fall into my drink as he leans over and laughs at something stupid I just said.

I casually slide my glass of water closer to myself, hoping he doesn't see me inspecting it for residue. "The new display looks beautiful," I say to distract him.

His dark brown eyes find mine and I see pride flicker through them. "Chocolate diamonds. They're gorgeous. Just gorgeous."

"What did it cost?"

He tilts his head to the side, gives me a look that he thinks is sly but with the light reflecting off his glasses I can only interpret the expression as awkward. Like he's momentarily blinded.

I clear my throat to cover the laugh that spills from my lips. "I'm thinking of getting a display for myself this season."

"Can you afford it?" he asks.

I try my best to dance around the question. "Things are looking good right now."

"Even with the money you'll shed on security?"

I sigh. "I may not end up getting security."

"Why not?"

"Haven't found anyone I like."

He watches me a moment, dark brows flattening on his forehead. "We agreed that you would either turn over the business or hire security."

Turn over weren't the terms I would use, but I ignore his words and just nod. "I know."

"Your safety is my top priority."

"Has our lawyer found anything?" I ask, trying to change the subject a little. We never got anywhere with the investigation. No arrests were made. No tips called in. I was stabbed in a dark alley in New York City, and no one knows who did it or why.

It was the same thing with the first assault years ago, except they at least had a suspect back then—Bobby. It didn't help that he completely disappeared but since he's shown up now without being arrested, I'm assuming his name has been cleared somehow. I never got involved with that case, I was only a teenager and between the assault and the sudden breakup, my parents didn't think I was mentally strong enough to handle the cops and detectives. I stayed focused on moving forward and getting through college.

I shiver as I try to concentrate on my brother's voice. "I worry about you. Are you taking your meds?" he asks.

I frown. "Don't ask me that, Grey."

He tsks. "I guess that's a no."

"My medication is honestly none of your business."

"As long as our family name is attached to your store, it is my business."

"So that's it?" I lean back in my chair. "It's all about the business. You don't really care about me."

"If you sink, there's a chance my business could suffer too. I'm just being honest."

"Your honesty stinks."

"Bri—"

I start gathering my purse, but he reaches out and grabs my wrist. It isn't rough at all, but I'm so angry, I jerk away and startle the waiter passing by. He stops and stares between us, unsure if he should intervene.

"We're fine," I say kindly.

He nods and walks away.

Greyson glowers. "Chill out. This is why I asked about the meds."

"I don't need the meds, Grey."

"Could have fooled me."

"I'm leaving," I say, slinging my purse onto my shoulder.

"Wait," he pleads.

"I'm not going to sit here while you insult me. I'm just as capable of running my store as you are of running yours."

"You've been different ever since the assault. The first one."

He's right. I spent the first year after Bobby disappeared bouncing from therapist to therapist, waking from night terrors, and moping around in tears. I was messed up to the point where my parents had no clue if I would ever be the same again.

By the grace of God, I did make it through college, and I set a goal to open my own jewelry store—which my parents helped fund as a congratulations for graduating with honors. Business has been tough, I'll admit that, but I'm positive I would have pulled things together in another year or two if I hadn't hit another bump in the road. This most recent attack has been more taxing than I thought it would be. And now Bobby's been thrown into the mix.

I huff and swipe at my curly bangs. "Who wouldn't be different after what I've experienced?" I say as loudly as I dare, not quite yelling. More like fierce whispering. "I was stabbed, Greyson. And your only concern is whether I'll ruin your precious reputation."

"My reputation *is* precious to me," he admits. "But so are you. That's why I installed the upgraded security system in your store, and the cameras, and why I offered to take the business off your hands."

"I'm not giving you my store," I say slowly. I'd rather get stabbed ten more times than hand my business over to Greyson.

I'll admit, *Grey Gems* is far more successful than Gem Jewelers, but we're not so bad that I'm willing to hand it over to Greyson of all people. That would be one more thing for him to hold over my head for the rest of my life, just like he's doing with the assault and the meds.

I sigh and adjust my purse on my shoulder. "I've really got to go, Grey."

He nods. "I'm only looking out for you."

32

I don't believe him for a second, but I'm also not in the mood to argue about it. I'd had a great night until that moment. I had even enjoyed myself enough to forget about my stressful day at the office. Now, I'm practically stomping out of the restaurant as I head to the exit. I don't have my phone, so I can't schedule an Uber from the app, thankfully, my apartment isn't too far from here and my shoes are comfortable.

I walk three blocks before I start puffing, my anger petering out and slowly getting replaced by fatigue. I'm *this* close to resting on the sidewalk when my building comes into view. I'm waiting at a light, panting from my trek through the city. There's a crowd around me, a couple sticking close, a woman with a dog, two teenagers who should probably be at home at this hour. There's also a man in the crowd. Tall and heavyset and standing far too close to me.

I casually inch away, and he respectfully gives me my space. The hairs on the back of my neck are all raised, but I smother my anxiety by focusing on the streetlight. The crowd shifts forward once it changes, but as I step off the curb, the man grabs me by the elbow and yanks me back.

I yelp as he jerks me toward him, slipping on the concrete, but there's another set of hands there to stable me.

Someone grabs my other arm and tugs me the other way, so I don't end up falling flat on my butt. At this point, I don't know who's attacking me and who's rescuing me, but the air is cleared when I glance up to find Bobby standing beside me.

The man who first grabbed me is just as bewildered as I am when he steps through the crowd. I expect a fight to break out. I expect Bobby to break that guy's face for touching me.

Instead, he very smoothly places an arm over my shoulders and turns me away. "Let's go," he says kindly but firmly.

I blink up at him, then I glance back at the man who's still on the curb watching us. "How—?"

"Just keep walking."

I pick up my pace. It's not like I'd rather stick around.

4

You could scold me for ignoring a woman when she tells you to leave her alone, but I think the fact that I just saved said woman from a certified creep should count for something.

Brianna is too busy glancing over her shoulder to realize that she's walking side by side with her ex-boyfriend. I'm grateful the freak across the street is still there leering at us because it makes the trip to her apartment much less awkward. With her attention focused elsewhere, Brianna doesn't notice that I've led her to her own front doors without her giving me any direction. That's right—I already know where she lives, as any good private security should, *ahem*.

I didn't show up in Bri's office with hope in my heart and a dream in my head. I walked in with a plan to get hired, so I did my research. In this day and age, anyone with access to good internet can find out the things I've learned. My lovely ex is an open book—always has been—and she loves social media. Her accounts are updated every few hours, which I assume is her attempt to build business by posting cute selfies on Instagram somehow. I mean ... I *do* follow her under a ghost account I created, but still. I don't care about her stupid diamonds; I care about *her*.

Yes. I said it. I care about Brianna Gem. I didn't roll out of bed and leave her six years ago because I'd gotten what I wanted from her. I left because I didn't have a choice.

Things are a lot more complicated between Brianna and me than she's led you to believe.

Well ... I *am* a scumbag. I can admit to that. Whatever my ex said about me during my high school years is true. Bobby Ackard wasn't the nice guy any decent man would have wanted near his sweet daughter. Which is why Bri's folks hated me.

I wasn't the prep school church boy they had in mind for their precious girl. I was a white trash thug who'd stolen his way into a school that was out of his league and charmed his way into the heart of a girl who was way too good for him. Despite where I'd come from, despite the rumors about my family being connected to the mafia, Brianna loved me. She *loved* me.

And I screwed everything up.

Like she's just now remembered this, Bri glances up at me as we reach the doors to her apartment complex. I can't get in without her key, so we stand awkwardly on the doorstep and blink at each other. She's still exactly as I remember her...

Angry.

"What are you doing here?" she hisses, pulling away from the arm I'd still had draped over her shoulders.

I sigh. "Gee, thanks for rescuing me, Bobby. You're

36

welcome, Brianna."

"I'm not thanking you for doing something you shouldn't have done."

"You do realize how ridiculous that sounds, right?"

Her gaze narrows until I feel like her eyeballs could cut me. "What are you doing here?"

"Following you." Might as well be honest.

"Why?"

"Because I wanted to speak with you."

"So you stalked me?"

"I was going to speak up when you got to your apartment, but that guy showed up—"

"Did you arrange that?"

I balk at her. "*What?*"

"Are you that desperate for my attention, Bobby? No means no." She turns and swipes her key across the door, it blinks green and unlocks—that's when I grab her by the elbow and drag her inside like the child she's decided to be tonight.

"Hey!" she squeals, but I ignore her and march to the elevator, punch the button with a grunt. It opens immediately and I tug her inside so hard she trips into me.

Her face is smooshed against my chest, so it takes her a moment to gather herself and push away. Our eyes meet with a snap, and I feel her hatred crackle around me, filling the small space with more negative energy than I can handle. Her anger comes off her in waves, so strong it robs me of words as I drown in her intensity.

Suddenly silenced, I turn and hit the button for the elevator doors to close. Once they're shut, I finally find the courage to speak. "Listen—"

"No, *you* listen—"

"I saved you!" I say sharply. "And you accuse me of setting all that up?"

"You walked into my office after how many years? Then you call my office. Then you stalk me. And it's all just to *talk*?"

"What else did you want me to do? You wouldn't have given me the time of day any other way."

She rolls her eyes, rubbing at her upper left arm. My eyes are immediately drawn to it. "Are you hurt?" I ask.

"No."

"Brianna—"

"What do you want, Bobby?"

"The job," I say plainly.

"For half the pay."

"I'll take twenty-five percent of the pay."

For some reason, this makes her angrier. Her brows flatten into one thick line and her pretty lips peel back into a snarl, but the elevator doors open before she can spew curses at me. The ding of our arrival stuns her into silence and she blinks dumbly into the hallway like she's never seen this place before.

I step out and hold my arm out for her to lead the way. "Can we talk about this inside?"

Without another word, Brianna brushes past me and makes a beeline for her apartment. We don't speak the entire walk, the only sound between us is our muffled footsteps against the thick carpet. Her place is expensive for someone managing a struggling business, but I don't comment on this. I doubt it'll do anything but raise more questions and cause another temper tantrum.

Honestly, I didn't have to do much research to find out about the state of her business. A trained eye could point out all the problems with her store as soon as you walk inside. My eyes aren't exactly trained, but I was her boyfriend for two years—I spent a lot of time in her father's shops staring at the diamonds I'd dreamed of buying her one day.

Gem Jewelers is nothing like her father's franchise, *Gemz*. All of her collections are outdated, the diamonds are pretty, but the cuts were in style five years ago. Her display looks cheap which makes the price tags seem like a rip off, especially when Jäger Diamonds is right down the street, selling rare gems and engagement rings like they're lollipops.

In Brianna's defense, Jäger Diamonds is a famous franchise that gives even her father's business a run for its money. I'm not surprised she's struggling to keep up with her little storefront just three blocks down from it. Part of their success is because the company faced a huge scandal back when we were in high school. The owners are ex mafia who went clean about ten years ago. The whole thing was all over the news, how the cops stormed New York City and chased the gangsters into hiding. The ones who weren't arrested made deals with prosecution and used all their drug money to open businesses.

How do I know all this? Because the rumors about my family are all true. We were connected to the mafia, right up until law enforcement took the city back. That's when things got complicated for my family. We weren't high-ranking mafia like the guys on the news who had millions of dollars to throw at lawyers or fly to safety out of the country. At that time, the Ackard name was still *Eckhardt*, and it belonged to a small German family who had served its Boss loyally. But when things went south, we went under.

My old man was arrested, my mother got a second job to pay for his lawyer. The cops traced our name back to the mafia—sending me and my brother away was all my mom could do to keep the police off our tails. My brother went with our grandparents while I changed my last name to Ackard and went to live with my aunt in Manhattan. She wasn't loaded but she did grow up on the right side of the law and had enough connections to get me into MA Prep where I met Brianna and all her rich friends.

Everything was fine for four years. And then it wasn't.

The lights flicker on in Brianna's apartment, startling me from my depressing thoughts. It looks exactly like what I would expect from a spoiled princess. Crème colored walls with warm, mocha toned carpeting. There are expensive tapestries on display, handwoven macrame designs that I know cost as much as the expensive coffee machine sitting pretty on her countertop. The appliances are all stainless steel, the kitchen is perfectly tiled, the living room holds a furniture set that looks like it belongs on the cover of a décor magazine for the rich and famous. But all of this is ruined by the pile of laundry on the sofa, the plates of half-eaten food on the kitchen counters, and—for some reason—the empty wine bottle that's resting in the sink.

Brianna tosses her keys into an artfully designed glass bowl and then sits on the barstool at the counter. She doesn't look me in the eye, just stares at her hands, intensely focused on her chipped nail polish while I stand awkwardly by the door.

She's embarrassed, I realize with a start. All her anger is gone now, her dark eyebrows no longer pinched together as she scowls, her full lips no longer arched into a frown. Her face is an image of dark emotions, but it isn't rage. It isn't bitter hatred.

I slowly move toward the counter, ignoring the mess around me, and sit beside her. This is the first time we've sat next to each other in years. I spend the moment of silence that stretches between us staring at the side of her face, searching for the teenager I left in the visage of the woman I've found.

Brianna is older now, more mature. Her eyes no longer dance with lust and intrigue, she isn't impressed with my 'bad boy' persona anymore. This Brianna is all about business in her nice clothes and nice shoes and the rich perfume I can smell from here. It's sweet and warm and makes something in my chest ache.

The rest of her is just the same, the curves of her body filling in to fit her womanly form. She isn't a little girl anymore and it certainly shows. The only thing that hasn't seemed to change much is Brianna's hair. It's always been wild and curly, and it still looks that way now, but there's a tameness to it that reminds me of a mane—like a kitten who's become a lion.

Something beeps beside me; I realize it's Brianna's watch

41

as she checks it and then taps a button. She casts me a sideways glance before reaching into her purse, when I hear a pill bottle rattling around, I stand and go to her fridge. I want to sigh when I peer inside, but I control myself and blink longingly at the empty shelves. There's nothing but a slice of cheese and a lonely can of Coke inside. I grab the soda and find a glass, once it's half full, I slide it across the counter to Bri.

She doesn't take it. I don't know if it's because she's embarrassed to take her medicine in front of me or because she's being stubborn, but I'm not just giving her a refresher for the night. She needs the drink for other reasons too.

"Your pupils are still dilated and you're breathing hasn't leveled out yet. You're still in shock," I tell her.

As if she's just realized this, Brianna clamps her hands together and takes three deep breaths. I slide the Coke closer. "Drink it, Bri. The sugar will help."

She takes the glass and sips; I turn away when I see the pills in her hands, giving her a few moments to toss them back without me watching.

"Thank you," she says over my shoulder.

I nod and turn back around. "You're welcome."

"You said you wanted to talk."

I suppose this is as close to a nice and calm conversation as I'm ever going to get with Bri. Might as well try to work things out now.

"I heard about the attack on the news," I say gently.

Just like that, whatever semblance of peace we'd established practically runs from the room. Brianna's face

42

scrunches in anger and she rises from her barstool. "Did you think you could come back and *protect* me?"

I give her a blank face. "Yes, Brianna. That's literally what my job entails."

"Why did you leave in the first place?"

I sigh. Now is not the time to go over this. I know she wants answers, I know she *deserves* answers, but it's the middle of the night and I just rescued her from a possible nutjob who may have wanted to harm or kill her.

"You're asking the wrong question," I say tiredly.

She quirks a single eyebrow.

"You shouldn't be wondering why I left, Bri. You should be asking why I've come back."

Her mouth opens and then closes. For the first time, she has nothing to say.

"Things were complicated when we were teenagers—they're still complicated now." I stare at her, trying to gage her emotions, trying to see behind the face of anger she's wearing. I can't get past the glare in her eyes. "Just know that I didn't leave because I wanted to."

Technically, I didn't come back because I wanted to, either. I missed Brianna, I really did, and I never wanted to leave her; but coming back has been just as hard as leaving. This is difficult for me too—the last six years of my life have been difficult. One big crap show that no one seems to care about because it's all about Princess Bri. The woman who got dumped like a cheap hooker.

I'm sorry for what I did, but I didn't have a choice. I still don't have a choice. But Brianna isn't ready to hear any of that. Right now, it's all about her broken heart. Not the crap I went through or the reasons I left—or the reasons I'm here now. I'm just her scumbag ex-boyfriend who's stumbled back into her life to remind her of all her broken memories.

I mean, seriously. Give me a break. Did you think I came into this story for *fun*?

Brianna might have been a good little Christian girl, but I wasn't the only one doing any influencing during our relationship. She had an effect on me to. My life was never peaceful, but it certainly wasn't so messy until I got involved with Princess Bri and her *wonderful* family.

They really were nice folks … On the surface.

Once you got past the plastic smiles and the firm handshakes, you saw the wrinkles in their faces and the claws beneath their fingers. Next thing I knew, my past was being thrown into my face and I had a choice to make. I thought I made the right one.

I was wrong.

Now that decision is still haunting me. Things are messed up right now. Really freaking messed up. And it seems like Brianna might be at the center of it all, but I'm not 100 percent certain yet. I don't want to say anything and get her unnecessarily worked up. But I'm not going to sit back and do nothing either. I did nothing six years ago and I paid dearly for that. This time around, I'm making sure I do things right.

The attack when we were teenagers. The attack two months ago. And then the creep on the street—whether our past has anything to do with it or not, I think it's safe to say that Brianna is being targeted. *Why* is something I'm still trying to figure out, but I've got some strong theories and everything that's happened to her recently is starting to piece it all together.

I look at her seriously. "I know I'm the last person you want to be around right now."

She nods without hesitation.

That stings but I shove away my emotions and keep going. "I'd like to give you the peace you desire, but you do need security, Bri. Tonight is proof of that."

"Do you seriously expect me to hire you?"

I step around the counter so I'm towering over her. She isn't a small woman, but I'm over six feet tall—I tower over everyone. "You want answers about what happened in our past. I'll give them to you."

"But only if I agree to hire you." She sighs. "What on Earth makes you think I'm desperate enough for answers that I'd give you a job just to get them?"

"You can't afford to hire anyone else but me. Let's be honest here."

She scowls at me.

"A quarter of the pay," I remind her.

Brianna looks away and folds her arms. I know she's going to give in before she says the words, but I'm surprised by them, nonetheless. "Alright," she mutters.

I smile. "I've got the job." It isn't a question.

"You've got the job." She pokes my chest, hard. "For *half*

the pay. We're not down bad enough to offer just a quarter of the deal."

I almost laugh. Yes, she is.

"And I want answers." Brianna looks me right in the eye, but there is no anger on her face like before. All I see in her expression is sorrow, it swells in her eyes as tears begin to gather. It's not until this moment that I realize the true weight of her pain, everything she's been holding in for the last six years.

I look away. "You'll get answers, Bri. I promise."

She clears her throat. "I have work tomorrow."

Obviously, that's my cue to leave.

I don't take offense to the abrupt ending to our night; I've just been hired as Brianna's private security; I'll be with her all day every day for the next six months. We've got plenty of time together from now on.

This should be fun.

5

I wake in a cold sweat, my worries and fears rolling down my forehead and dripping off my chin. My nightmares usually feature the man who attacked me two months ago, but last night I dreamed of the stranger from the street corner. I don't want to think of what could have happened if Bobby hadn't shown up when he did, but I also don't want to address the fact that he did show up. This changes everything—and not just because I'm working with my ex-boyfriend now. It changes things because his presence forces me to acknowledge just how messed up things are.

I've been attacked three times now. Unprovoked. By a complete stranger. Granted, this is New York City… Anyone could get taken down by a deranged hobo as much as a thug with a pocketknife. But I wasn't attacked by either type of lunatic.

The first guy was a man who swiped at me and Bobby while we were out together on a date. The second was a faceless man who stabbed me outside my own jewelry store.

The last guy was just a random dude who got a little grabby. Any one of those men could have been thugs looking to rob someone who appeared to have money.

My store may not be doing as well as I'd like right now, but I'm still a member of the Gem family. Our franchise is known across the country, that makes it totally plausible for someone to have recognized me and thought they could rob me in the street.

It sounds a little farfetched, but it isn't totally impossible. Whatever the case, I'm determined to do something about this. I'm tired of constantly feeling on edge, I'm tired of my shaking hands and frazzled nerves. This won't end until the guys who've attacked me are behind bars.

My watch chimes, startling me from my daydreams. I wipe my sweat and climb over my fluffy blankets to get to my bedside table. Last night was rough, I actually gave in and took my pills and then fell asleep with guilt pressing down on my chest.

Today, I'm going to start over.

I turn off my alarm and slide down the side of the bed, so I land on my knees. My morning prayers roll off my tongue like a mantra I've whispered time and again. Admittedly, I'm not someone who prays often, but if I'm starting over I may as well do it right. There's a Bible in my bedside table, I take it out and read through one of my favorite passages, but as I slide it back into the top drawer, I catch a glimpse of my journal. The one with the dreaded sticky note stuck to the last page.

My throat begins to close as tears spring to my eyes. The

sudden emotion is unwanted and unwarranted. I like to pride myself as a strong, independent woman, but that's just a front for my trendy posts on social media. This is the real me, a little girl who can barely make it out of bed without crying.

I take a deep breath and shut the drawer. I'm not looking forward to dealing with Bobby today, but at least I have the morning to myself. The store doesn't open until 9 a.m., right now it's only 7. That's at least another hour and a half to myself.

A smile works its way over my face, replacing the sorrow from earlier. An hour and a half gives me the time to shower, eat, wrestle my hair into submission, and pick out a nice outfit. If I hurry, I could beat Bobby to the store and explain things to Lyla before she sees him. I have no idea what to expect today… this hour of solitude is my only reprieve, the only time I'll have to prepare myself for what's to come. I thank God for every second—

And then I open my bedroom door and find Bobby in my kitchen.

I freeze in place, my jaw falling open as I rub at my eyes. When my vision clears up, Bobby is still there, dressed in a casual t-shirt and jeans, moving through my cabinets like he owns the place. I smell coffee and eggs and toast, and I try hard to ignore the sudden pangs of hunger that claw through my stomach.

The last time I saw Bobby, I'd said goodbye to him at my front door and then closed and locked it behind me. Now he's making breakfast in my apartment like a hired chef—no—like a live-in lover. He's even humming to himself as he checks the toast and sets it on a plate to serve.

Sunlight splashes in from the window over the stove, crashing over him in a violent storm of luminescent sunshine. It lights up every part of him, his golden blonde hair and suntanned skin; he is perfectly calm and relaxed as he works, not like a security guard who saved me from a strange man last night.

That guy had been the Bobby I remembered. The teenager with an attitude who wasn't afraid to throw a punch at anyone who looked at him the wrong way. Every muscle in his body had been rigid as he'd led me to safety, reminding me that Bobby was only the same boy in his mind and in his memories, not in his body or his form. Even now, I see the difference between the eighteen-year-old who'd charmed me and the twenty something man before me.

He is taller, leaner, his body now mature and taking on a man's physique. There are tattoos along his arms that weren't there when we were kids, bold black lines zigzagging across his skin. If you look close enough, you can see the scars they cover, evidence of the sort of life he's lived these last six years.

Suddenly, he glances up and notices me still standing by my door. A grin claims his perfect lips, curving upward ever so slightly. "Good morning."

"Why are you in my apartment?" I fold my arms over my chest, but not because I'm angry, it's because I'm standing here in nothing but an oversized sleepshirt. No bra. "How'd you even get in?"

"I took your keys before I left."

"You what?"

He shrugs and scoops eggs onto a plate. "I can't guard you properly from the lobby, Bri."

"I thought you'd meet me at the store."

"And what would happen if someone attacked you on the way there?"

I frown. "I can handle getting to work on my own."

"Just like you can handle getting home on your own?"

That was a low blow, but I choose not to respond. Instead of snapping at him, I turn toward the bathroom with a huff.

Bobby calls out to me. "Where are you going?"

"To shower."

"Your eggs will get cold." He sighs behind me. "I bought them fresh this morning."

"I'll just have coffee. Thanks."

The kitchen is nice and clean when I finally emerge from the bathroom, steam rolling out behind me. Bobby is sitting on the couch beside a neatly folded pile of laundry. I shouldn't be upset that he cleaned my space and loaded up my fridge, but I am. It feels like he's trying to buy my friendship and my only response is controlled anger.

"Why did you let yourself into my apartment?" I say as calmly as I can. "I could have been walking around naked this morning."

"I thought you heard me out here cooking and cleaning."

"You're not a maid, you're a security guard."

"I don't want to live in a pigsty."

"*Live?*" My face crinkles in both confusion and rage. "You're not living here, Bobby!"

Now he looks confused. "How else am I supposed to protect you all day?"

I want to rip my hair out.

"You can stand outside the door. I'll scream if I need something."

Bobby stares at me, nonplussed. "You're being a little stubborn, don't you think?"

My nostrils flare. "Let me make this clear to you. I don't want you here. I don't want to be around you. I don't even want to look at you. But I'm starting to believe my life is in danger, and you might know why. I want answers and I want your protection—what I don't want, or *need*, is your friendship."

I expect him to rise to his feet in anger, to give me lip about my attitude and demand an apology or a thank-you for cleaning my apartment. Instead, I'm gifted with one of Bobby's crooked grins as he quirks a single blonde eyebrow. He does rise to his feet, standing so tall I have to take a step back, but the action isn't intimidating—it somehow has the opposite effect, like he's drawing me in.

My ears begin to burn as I blink up at him, but I don't find the courage to speak. Suddenly, all the spunk and attitude I had before is gone, chased out of the room by Bobby's blistering gaze.

"What's it going to take for me to get on your good side, Princess?"

I bristle. "I got *attacked*, Bobby! Six years ago, you brought that drama into my life and now it's back—as soon as you show up again."

He frowns, his searing gaze turning ice cold. "What are you insinuating, Brianna?"

"You said you have answers," I remind him.

He nods.

"Is it because you've been playing a part in all this?"

Shock storms over Bobby's face, conquering his features. Even though he looks like he wants to snap at me, his voice comes out gently, little more than a whisper. "Is that what you really think?" His eyes drop to the floor. "That I would ever hurt you?"

"Y—You're dangerous, Bobby."

He blinks at me, blue orbs shutting off then on almost mechanically. I can see the effect my words have had, the way he takes a slow step back like he doesn't want to be near me anymore. It's a tiny gesture but it shifts the mood in the entire room.

One of the things Bobby has always feared is being condemned. Being cast aside because of his family, judged for sins he's never committed. It's a fear that runs deep—deeper than I will ever know. He was chased out of his home because the police had judged him, he was treated as an outcast in school because the students judged him. Even my family hated him because of unwarranted judgment. It was a fear that'd eaten him alive as a teenager, and I'd just thrown it in his face.

The last time I saw Bobby, we were in love. I was the only

53

one who didn't care about his family's ties or the rumors of his connection to the mafia. To call him dangerous now, to even hint that I would blame him for anything that's happened to me... the accusation is like a slap in the face.

The look on his face alarms me, serious yet wary—like he isn't sure if he should prepare a snappy comeback or guard himself from my next words. The idea that anything I have to say could ever hurt him almost leaves a lump in my throat.

You can't hurt someone who doesn't give a crap about you. But I don't want to think about the fact that Bobby Ackard *could* give a crap, that he *could* actually care. Because if he'd ever cared he wouldn't have brought danger to my doorstep and left as soon as things got hot. *He saved himself because he only cares about himself.*

His words from last night run through my head, almost in his defense. *I didn't leave because I wanted to.*

I squeeze my eyes shut and shake my head, startled by the warmth that blooms on my arm. "Bri?" Bobby is touching me, leaning down to look into my eyes.

"I'm fine." I shake him off.

"You think I'm dangerous," he prods.

"I don't know what I think. I want to go to the police," I say quietly.

"You what?"

"I was attacked last night. I want to file a report—"

"That's not going to do anything, Bri."

"It'll leave a paper trail. And it will get the police involved."

He crosses his arms over his broad chest, I ignore the cords of muscle that twist and flex with the motion. "Did the police catch the first guy or the guy from two months ago?"

"No—"

"And somehow you think they'll catch this guy."

"I think reporting him is the right thing to do."

He shakes his head. "I don't."

"Why not?"

"Because it will just alert the culprit—give him a heads-up that police are after him. All he'll do is lay low until the cops lose interest, and in a city like New York, they'll lose interest quite fast."

"No, they won't." He starts to sigh but I talk right over him. "My uncle is Police Commissioner, with his niece being attacked twice in two months, police will definitely do something."

Bobby knows this is true; my uncle's position in law enforcement is one of the reasons my family hated him so much. Back in high school, before he became Commissioner, my parents feared Bobby's place in my life would negatively impact my uncle's chances of getting the promotion. Of course, I had disagreed, but then I was attacked, and Bobby took off. The problem seemed to have fixed itself.

And now it's back again.

"Let me do my own investigation," Bobby offers.

His words snap my vision toward him. "You're not a cop."

"Which means I'm not restricted by any laws."

My brows lower. "There are laws you still have to follow."

"And I'll try my best to follow them."

I don't like the sound of this at all. "Bobby, I didn't hire you to become a detective."

"You hired me to protect you. That'll be much easier to do if I know who's after you and why."

I sigh, hating how much sense he's making right now. "Promise me one thing."

He nods, almost eagerly.

"You will stay in your place. That means no more cooking breakfast in my kitchen. No more trying to be friends. You're my security guard. Nothing more."

He nods again, this time a little less enthusiastically. "Alright, Bri, I promise."

I eye him for an extra moment which makes him smile crookedly.

"I said I promise." He places a hand over his heart. "I'm not leaving your side, but I'm good enough at my job to keep to the shadows. You won't even know I'm there."

I sigh tiredly. Somehow, I don't believe a word he just said.

6

Brianna keeps glancing over her shoulder as we walk the last block to her store. At first, I thought it was because she was still spooked from what happened to her with that grabby creep, but as her eyes scan the area with a wild look of wonder swirling in them, I realize she's looking for me.

I almost chuckle. She's made it more than clear that she doesn't want me around, and now that I've kept up my promise to stay hidden, she's searching the Manhattan crowd for me. I'm only a few paces behind, far enough to give her some privacy but close enough to intervene if there's trouble. She should be able to spot me in the mass of walking bodies, not because my hair is so blonde or my eyes are so blue—but because I'm literally a head taller than almost everyone else around me. But I wouldn't be very good security if I were that easy to spot, even at my height.

The key to blending in is to act like you aren't trying to. I pretend I'm just another guy walking to work with the rest of the folks around me, checking my phone at the right intervals and minding my business. I do have to hunch my shoulders a little so I'm not sticking straight up out of the crowd. But other than my attempt at making myself seem shorter, the only effort I put into staying hidden is purposely acting normal.

Brianna never spots me. I don't expect her to, but I also don't expect the scowl she casts into the crowd as she takes one last look over her shoulder before heading into the store. She's upset that she couldn't spot me.

That's interesting.

I pull out my phone and send her a text. **I'm right outside, Princess.**

She texts back right away. **Not coming in?**

I don't feel the need to follow her inside, the store is rather small—small enough for me to see most of the place through the floor-to-ceiling display windows. I'd rather stand guard out here, walk a few blocks and circle back to see if there are any suspicious looking guys hanging around.

Nah, the job's easier out here. But I'm flattered you miss me already.

I just *know* she's rolling her eyes now.

What if something happens inside?

Then I'll come in and kick someone's a—I stare at my phone, frowning. I'm not sure how Bri would feel about me using foul language around her. We weren't little angels in high school, but she had always tried to take her faith seriously. All while I'd tried my best to pry her King James Bible from her manicured hands. I had succeeded in many ways. Trading her Bible for a pack of cigarettes and her cotton panties for lacy thongs. By the time we graduated, there wasn't much we hadn't done together. And before I left, we'd finally checked the last thing off our list.

Go ahead. Judge me. I know you already have anyway.

We were kids. Church rules weren't any fun or of any importance back then. But things have changed now; the attacks, the breakup, my poorly timed return. I wonder what else is different now. If Brianna's gotten herself together spiritually, if she takes all that God stuff seriously now.

I don't. And I haven't changed.

But this story isn't really about me, is it?

I delete the text and send a different one. **If something happens, I'll be right here.**

How do I know that?

I can't tell if she's hinting at the fact that I've been MIA for the last six years or if she's genuinely concerned because she has no idea where I'm at right now.

I'm not going anywhere, Bri.

She doesn't respond for a few minutes, and I debate sending another message—**Not again.** But that seems like overkill. It's a miracle she trusts me enough to hire me, I don't want to push the boundaries too far too soon, especially after I just promised to keep things professional and friendly with her.

My phone buzzes in my hand. **Ok.**

One little word. It holds the weight of our entire relationship right now. An admittance of trust? Or just a momentary agreement that you believe what I just told you?

I cram my phone into my pocket and glance up at the storefront. The lights are all on, casting spotlights on the display boxes, diamond rings sparkling inside glass cases. I can see Brianna moving through the store, getting things set up for the day, there's a focused look on her face and a determined pep in her step. This is a side of her I haven't seen before, but I'm not surprised by her demeanor. She's a businesswoman now, her own boss. I missed all the joys of the last six years—her graduating from college, deciding she wanted to follow in her old man's footsteps. Taking out a business loan, picking out a building.

Those are things we would have done together if I had been here.

I shake my head and start walking down the street. It doesn't matter what I missed because I'm here now and I'm determined to make things better. I have no idea how to do that but getting Brianna to trust me again is certainly a good place to start. That somehow feels like it will be the most difficult task of them all—even harder than catching her masked assailant. Probably because she's convinced I know the assailant.

That's one thing that hasn't changed in all this time. Brianna still thinks I had something to do with what happened to her in high school. *Everyone* still thinks I had something to do with it. What they've all forgotten is that the thug who robbed us pointed a knife in *my* face too. I didn't just freeze up because he was my buddy and we'd finally managed to corner the Gem Princess—I froze because I was an eighteen-year-old kid standing face to face with a man who wanted to kill me for simply existing.

I still remember every detail of that day as if it happened just last night. Brianna and I had been out with our friends, but I had to get her home by a certain time because it was Saturday—she had church the next day and I'd promised I would go with her and her family. We were running late, and she was afraid she would miss her curfew, so I took us down an alley as a shortcut.

That was the worst decision I've ever made.

Halfway down the alley, we heard the voice behind us. As if he'd literally been hiding in the shadows, a man peeled from the wall—a spot we'd just passed—and held up a knife. We could have turned to run, we should have run, but neither Brianna nor I could move at all. It all felt so surreal, like I was watching it happen to someone else instead of experiencing it myself.

The man stepped forward into the moonlight, giving us a good look at his tan face and the puckered scar stretched across his cheek. His vision had been focused on Bri, but when I stepped in front of her, his attention shifted.

I remember the moment recognition claimed his features, eyes widening—the scar on his cheek tugging upwards as he smiled. All his teeth were rotten.

"You're an Eckhardt."

I didn't reply.

"This ain't Brooklyn, boy. This here is Moreno territory."

He was right. Back when the mafia ruled New York, each

gang had full control over an individual borough. The Russian Bratva ruled Staten Island under the Volkov family, the Italian mob ruled Manhattan through the De Luca house, dozens of smaller gangs came together to reign over the Bronx under one organization. The leader of this group was named Jameson Willis and he called his organization the Willis Stronghold. Meanwhile, the Spanish mafia ruled Queens under the Moreno head family, and the German mafia had control over Brooklyn through the Jäger dynasty.

That's where my family came from, where I had been born and raised until the police stormed the city and began making arrests left and right. Mafiosi were dragged to prison—high and low ranking men and women, those who weren't arrested either fled the country or turned on their gangster brothers, making deals with prosecution so they wouldn't have to serve time.

In the end, all five gangs fell, but there were still petty criminals on the streets who tried to keep the mafia culture alive. People like the man who had a knife to me and my girlfriend, claiming a German like myself had no business roaming the streets of Queens—Spanish territory.

"The gang wars are over," I'd tried to reason with him. The mafia had fallen nearly four years ago at the time, back when I was just a freshman in high school. But my words had no effect on the man before me. He didn't care that the Morenos had been run out of New York, that the Jägers had packed up and left years ago. That the mafia was dead.

To him, I was a grimy German in the wrong place at the

wrong time. For whatever reason, that meant Brianna had to pay.

He glanced over my shoulder at Bri who'd been cowering behind me the whole time. I could feel her clutching the back of my shirt, balling the material into her fist. Her hand shook against me, reminding me that there was more at risk than my own safety.

"You want money?" I said to the man, reaching into my pocket.

He yelled, "Don't move!"

"I'm just reaching for my wallet."

"I said *don't move*." In one swift motion, the man lunged forward and grabbed me by the shirt. Brianna yelped as he slammed me into the wall. I felt the prick of the knife against my neck as he pressed it into my flesh. That's when it all became real to me. That I was about to be robbed by an angry hobo in a dark alley, and there was nothing I could do about it. He could have *killed* me and there was nothing I could do except stare at the knife as it glinted in the moonlight.

He pointed it right in my face as he checked my pockets, but he didn't need to brandish the weapon. I was frozen stiff, shock and fear pouring into my mind, my heart, and my body. My legs seemed to stiffen with every second that passed, until it felt like I weighed a thousand pounds.

I didn't move when the man grabbed Brianna by the hair and shoved her to the ground. I didn't move when he started unzipping his pants. Only the sound of her shrieking brought me back, but by then, she had already decided to fight for herself.

She kneed the man hard in the groin, dropping him to the ground so she could claw at his face. All he could do was scream and flail—Brianna was quite scary when she was angry, and right then, she was outraged.

I should have been outraged. *I* should have been the one stomping on that guy's face, but it was Brianna instead. I had just gotten *robbed,* and my girlfriend had almost been raped right in front of me—and all I'd done was stand there.

Brianna grabbed my arm as she turned to run, the man had clambered to his feet, taking an angry swipe at us as we sprinted off. I heard her scream, but I didn't realize the knife had gotten her until we stopped a few blocks away. That's when I noticed the blood soaking the back of her shirt. We went to the hospital where her parents and the cops were notified.

That's when everything changed.

As soon as Colonel Gem heard that I'd stood and watched while his daughter had fought for her life and virtue, he started pointing fingers. The fact that the man had mentioned my family name and pretty much accused me of being part of the German mafia immediately made police suspicious of me. Before I knew it, they were saying I was the number one suspect. That I'd planned the whole thing with a gangbanger friend, that I'd tried to rob the Gem Princess after some late-night partying.

Brianna didn't stand up for me. She didn't try to correct her parents, didn't try to dispel the rumors that I was a thug who'd turned on his own girlfriend. Chosen the mafia over his lover.

When I confronted her about the whole thing, she looked me right in the eye and said she had no idea what to believe.

"You stood there, Bobby. You watched him hurt me. And you would have watched him kill me if I hadn't fought for myself."

She was right. But not because I was working with the guy who'd attacked us. I stood there because I was *scared*, just as scared as she had been. But when you're a rebellious teen with a bad attitude from the wrong side of the tracks, you don't get to be afraid. You don't get to freeze up. That was when I was supposed to let loose, bash that guy's face in like the lowlife bloodthirsty thug they thought I was.

"Is that what you wanted from me?" I had asked her. "To act just like them, right? Be the thug I've always been."

She never answered.

For weeks, I avoided Brianna, trying to give her and her family some space. The news finally stopped reporting on the assault, but the investigation never stopped. The cops brought me in for questioning four times, each time it became clearer that they wanted me in jail—whether I was innocent or not. I was an Eckhardt, and the Gem heiress and niece of the Captain of NYPD had been attacked in an alley while I'd stood and watched.

This was vengeance. This was justice for all the real mafiosi who fled the city and evaded arrest. For all the big-name bosses who didn't serve the time they deserved. The cops had gotten the city back, had pried the reins from the clawed hands of the mafia, but hardly any mafia paid for the crimes they committed. Even the queen of the German mafia had been arrested for murder and was released after serving just two months in jail.

Getting me behind bars would make the city feel safe again. Make the cops feel proud of themselves. It didn't matter that I was just a kid who'd been a victim too, it didn't matter that the Eckhardt family was small and relatively detached from the mafia. We were German and we'd been connected to the Jägers at one point. That was all anyone needed to call me guilty.

When I saw Brianna again, it was at her request. She'd invited me to her graduation party, and then asked if we could talk afterward. Only then did I get any sense or hint that she still cared, but the damage had been done. Our trust had been broken. I could see the doubt in her eyes when I told her I was innocent. I could see the poison planted by her parents working its way from her mind to her heart.

She was closing me out. Turning against me.

"Don't do this, Bri," I had whispered. I'd snuck into her bedroom that night once the guests had left the party. I was determined to convince her that I still loved her and that she was still my girl. "You have to believe me."

She'd sobbed, clutching at my chest as I'd held her. "I want to believe you."

"You know I'd never hurt you."

"I know."

"You know how much I love you."

"I love you too."

"Do you?" I pulled away, looking her right in the eye,

searching for the stars that used to dance in her gaze whenever she blinked up at me.

All I saw was worry and fear, but as I leaned down to kiss her, I caught a glimpse of something else. Something darker.

Desire.

No ... it wasn't love anymore. But the wanting was still there. The passion was still there. The aching need to be close to one another—that had never faded, despite the rumors and the allegations. Brianna still wanted me, and I was willing to settle for that.

We made love for the first time with her parents right next door. Bunched the blankets up on the floor so we didn't rock the bed. It wasn't romantic, it didn't even feel meaningful. But it was done. I had taken a part of Brianna that no man could ever have, not the thug from the alley, or whatever gentleman waltzed his way into her life after I climbed out her bedroom window that night. It hadn't been love, but it had been enough.

I got arrested the next morning.

The cops came to my house, but everything went down quietly—out of respect for the Gem family and Captain Jerome Lee—Bri's uncle—no reporters or news cameras were involved. They claimed they wanted everything settled quickly and quietly to protect Brianna's reputation, but I knew the truth. They wanted everything done hush-hush because I was innocent. And because Colonel Gem knew if his daughter ever found out he had me arrested with no evidence, she would never forgive him.

I went to jail for four years for a crime I didn't commit.

Convicted of assault with a deadly weapon, gang involvement, and attempted rape—and the entire time, Brianna thought I'd abandoned her. Thought I'd taken what I wanted and then dipped like she'd never mattered to me. She had no idea I was in jail. Had no idea that I was just as alone and heartbroken as she was.

When I got out, I had every intention to make things right with her, but Colonel Gem himself was there to congratulate me on my early release. He wasn't happy for me; he'd only shown up to let me know who'd pulled the strings to get me out five years before time.

"And I can put you back in just as easily," he'd said with a pat on my back. "Get out of town and don't come back, Robert. Ever."

I did leave, and I would have swallowed my pride and my anger and stayed gone if it weren't for Brianna's second attack.

The first one, when we were teens, was something I couldn't have predicted. But the second one... No one gets stabbed in an alley twice without at least one of them being a targeted assault.

That's what brought me back. A desire to prove my innocence, and to protect Brianna.

Think about it. Her parents hated me, and her uncle couldn't stand me. I was a threat to Captain Lee's chances at becoming Commissioner and I was a stain on the Gem's otherwise pristine reputation. They all wanted me gone—all except Brianna. She was the wrench in whatever plan they had going. It wouldn't have been enough to simply pin whatever crime on me and toss me in jail. They had to turn Brianna against me, or else she'd never stop fighting for my release.

That's exactly what happened. I lost Bri's trust in that alley, and I lost her heart when I 'disappeared' the morning after taking her virginity. She's never forgiven me, and she's never stop thinking I had something to do with what happened that night. Now that she's been attacked again, with me showing my face in town once more, her beliefs about that whole event are just being solidified.

Brianna's been assaulted twice in the last two months. Maybe I'm wrong. Maybe I wasn't set up by her family. But someone wants to hurt Bri. If I can't use these six months to prove my innocence, then I'll use them to stop whoever's going after her. That's the least I can do. She may never trust me again, but I hope this will be enough to earn her forgiveness.

7

Bobby's been quiet lately. Exactly one week of our arrangement and we haven't gotten into an argument. It's strange and slightly unsettling, but not just because we've managed not to kill each other. It's weird because I'm bothered by his silence.

True to his word, Bobby's made himself sparce. I hardly notice he's around unless he appears by my side like a shadow stepping from the wall. Sometimes he gets a kick out of startling me, but other than an angry scowl at his joking, I barely interact with him. He doesn't offer conversation on our walks to and from work, when I get home, he stands outside the door as promised, and if I've got somewhere else to go, I just send him a text and he slides into the shadows like he was never there from the start.

Even last night when I had dinner with Greyson again, I never saw or heard anything from Bobby. I searched for him, which has become something of a game for me when I'm bored at work. I'll stare out my window, blinking at the passing shoppers, craning my neck to glance down the street as I polish my jewelry at the display box. But I never see Bobby. Not until he wants to be seen.

It's an odd thing to feel absolutely safe and secure yet scared out of your mind at the same time. I'm still not sure I can trust Bobby, still unsure what his presence in my life means now, but I can't deny that having him around has made things easier. I'm not as anxious as I used to be, my hands aren't constantly shaking—I've even cut back on the meds, which has made my mother proud.

Mama Shelly gave me a tight hug when I joined her in church this last Sunday. After making it through yet another random NYC assault, I feel like I've got a lot to be thankful for—plus, going to church always helps put my mom in a good mood. Even Bobby went with me, though he waited outside. I sent him a text asking him to join us in the sanctuary, but he didn't even bother texting back. The stubborn side of me refused to be offended, the small bit of peace between us is not the same as making amends. Bobby isn't even here to make amends. He's here because he's hired help.

Hired help or not, I grunt internally, *he promised me some answers.*

It's one o'clock in the afternoon on a Tuesday and I'm walking the busy Manhattan streets with a growling stomach and no plan in mind. I have an hour and a half for lunch, thanks to Lyla packing her own food and agreeing to keep the shop for an extra thirty minutes. Bobby is somewhere behind me, but I'm not sure he'll follow me inside the sandwich shop at the next corner. Most days, I have lunch in my office or if I leave to eat with Lyla, he keeps his distance and remains unseen. I have no idea when he eats—or *if* he eats—but today I've decided he's at least going to sit with me.

I pull out my phone as I enter the sandwich shop. **Come in with me.**

It beeps with a response while I'm ordering two sandwiches and a basket of fries. **No.**

Bobby, don't be stubborn.

I don't eat with clients.

Really? I scan the crowd outside as I take a seat by the window, holding up one of the sandwiches—because I know he's watching. **I bought you food. Don't waste it.**

A few seconds later, Bobby appears like magic, stepping from beneath the awning of a nearby fruit stand. He crosses the street at a slow jog, blonde locks bouncing against his shoulders. Like usual, he's wearing plain jeans and a simple tee. Aside from his good looks, there is nothing particularly special about Bobby's appearance; he honestly looks like a copy of every other guy I've passed on the street. Even though he's tall and his arms are lined with black ink, I've never been able to point him out in public.

He slides into the seat across from me and sighs. "Trying to buy my love with food, Princess?"

I roll my eyes. "We aren't even friends, why would I ever try to buy your love?"

The grin on his face withers into a scowl as he grabs one of the sandwiches. "What's up with the lunch, then?"

"We've been getting along this past week—"

"Because we haven't been communicating except for the occasional text."

"Right." I pick up a fry. "But I think we've gotten along enough to manage a decent conversation."

He bites his sandwich and then licks a bit of mustard from the corner of his mouth. I shamelessly watch the action, his tongue sliding out to graze his lips. That's when I notice the crumbs on his chin, tiny morsels of bread that stand out against his otherwise perfect jaw.

I'm suddenly struck with an urge to reach out and wipe the food away, to feel his skin beneath my fingertips. It stirs up a memory of me doing exactly that during a lunch with our friends—Bobby had always been a sloppy eater. But just as I'd wiped the food away, he'd grabbed my wrist and held my hand in place so he could kiss my fingers one by one.

It takes an embarrassing amount of effort to keep my hands to myself now. I blink away the memory and focus on Bobby's sharp blue eyes as he pierces me with his focused gaze.

"What sort of conversation are we about to have?" he asks. There is caution in his voice.

"I have questions and you promised answers."

He groans, reaching for the basket of fries. "Do we have to do this right now?"

"I need to know, Bobby. You owe me that much."

"Fine. But can we at least start with simple questions first?"

I glance down at my untouched food. "Fine."

"Shoot." He taps the table, drawing my eyes to his hand. There's a scar on his thumb, and as he reaches to grab more fries, I realize it wraps around his hand and continues over his palm—like he was slashed while holding his hands up. Defending himself.

His left hand has a tattoo on each finger, a star, a thorn, a crown, and a bullseye on the knuckle of his middle finger. I see another bullseye on the inside of his wrist, that one is harder to make out in the sea of ink that crawls up his arm. He's got ink going up to his shoulders, even poking out the collar of his t-shirt to dance along his neck.

"Why all the tats?" I ask.

Bobby slowly pulls his arm toward himself and rests it under the table. "It's been a long six years."

What sort of answer is that?

"What do they mean?"

He sighs and holds his hand up so I can see the designs on his fingers. "The star of David, the thorn and crown represent the 'thorny crown' from Christ's crucifixion."

"I don't remember you being so religious," I tease.

He chuckles. "I needed all the help I could get when I was in—" he cuts himself off, even flicks his gaze away, jaw locking in frustration.

"In where?" I ask.

He takes a breath. "Not now, Bri."

It isn't the answer I want, but I know if I pry any deeper, he'll shut down completely. I can't have that—I've still got more questions.

My eyes land on the bullseye tattoo.

"What about that one?"

He glances at his middle knuckle. "That one..."

From the tone of his voice, I already know what it means.

Back when the mafia ruled New York, the German gangs were led by the Jäger family—*Jäger* means Hunter in their native tongue. One of the signs affiliated with the Hunters of New York was the bullseye, like their own little logo. Throughout high school, there were a few guys who got the bullseye tattoo just to seem tough, but the ink on Bobby's skin doesn't seem like a show or an act.

I can't stop myself from thinking of all the rumors surrounding Bobby's involvement in the mafia. As kids, we'd ignored the whispers; he was German and rebellious—that was all anyone needed to start saying he was a thug. I'd never believed the rumors, not until the day I got stabbed in an alley and he'd watched.

Now he's got bullseyes tattooed onto his skin in multiple places, and he doesn't want to talk about it.

"Bobby," I say slowly, "I need answers."

"I know."

"I need to know the truth."

He looks at me with an expression I can't put into words. "Are you asking if I'm mafia, Brianna?"

I frown. "I'm asking what really happened that night. Why did you come back after six years? What do you know about everything that's been plaguing my life?" I push my sandwich away. "I just want to know. I deserve to know."

"I agree," he says calmly. "But are you ready to know, Bri? Can you accept the truth?"

"What does that mean?"

"It means things are more complicated than you realize. I told you I didn't leave because I wanted to." He leans forward, and it's so sudden that I jerk backwards in my chair, making it scrape along the tiled floor. A few heads turn at the screeching noise, but Bobby ignores them, his attention focused entirely on me. "I wasn't done with you or bored of you, Brianna. I loved you back then." His voice drops to a whisper, though his eyes never leave mine. "I still do."

I stand, appetite gone. "Alright—"

"Bri, wait—"

I turn and start toward the exit, ignoring the sound of his chasing footsteps. By the time my feet hit the sidewalk, Bobby's right beside me, his hand reaching for mine. I yank it away and start marching down the street.

"Wait!" he calls, walking beside me again—this time, he doesn't try to touch me. "What's wrong?"

"I need *answers* not affection!" I fold my arms like a child just to keep myself from accidentally touching him. I'm not repulsed by Bobby; I'm repulsed by the effect his affection is having on me.

I can feel it deep inside me, a knot of emotion unfurling, a yearning for his touch, a desire to feel his nearness once again. He just confessed to loving me—after six years of silence, after disappearing on the night we first made love. After I had found it in my heart to forgive him for standing there while I fought for my life. And just like that, my heart leapt at the opportunity to forgive him once again. To start over. To love him as passionately and fiercely as I had as a teenager.

But I can't.

It's not fair. It's not right. Bobby doesn't deserve my love, my heart, or my forgiveness. Not after everything he's done. I have scars from that night. I have fears I can't face. I have nightmares that play on repeat every time I close my eyes. And it's all because of him.

Were my parents right? Had Bobby's rebellious past finally caught up with him and dragged me into it? Or was Bobby innocent? Had he left for reasons too painful to discuss?

I gasp as I wipe at my eyes, still trying to walk even though I can barely see through my tears. I don't need to deal with these emotions right now. I just need the truth.

I stop walking to glare at Bobby, not caring about my mascara running down my cheeks. I hope he sees what he's reduced me to. I hope he knows it's all his fault.

He stares at me, as shocked as he is concerned.

"If you don't have answers, then don't speak to me," I say venomously.

"Brianna—"

I shake my head. "You are hired help, Bobby. Not my friend. Not my lover. Answers—*that's* what I want from you. Until you're ready to talk, we aren't talking at all."

A muscle in his jaw tics as he clenches it, but his words come out in a voice as calm as still water. "As you wish, Princess."

His words send shards of ice digging into my heart. I welcome the bitter cold because it's better than the scorching heat—the burning passion that keeps trying to rise between us.

"The next time I ask you a question, I expect you to tell me the truth. I'm ready for it. I can handle it."

He nods. "As you wish."

Without another word, I turn and march down the street toward the store.

8

Brianna and I haven't spoken in three days. We don't need to speak for me to get the job done—in fact, I think things are better this way. After that last argument, where she yelled at me in the middle of the street, I'm done trying to get on her good side. I served her my heart on a platter, and she stabbed it with her butter knife. And then blamed me for it all!

I told her it wasn't the right time to have that conversation. I said I didn't want to answer her questions or talk about my tattoos. Brianna wants the truth, but she can't handle it, and every time she's faced with that fact, she falls back on the blame game. Everything's *my* fault.

I broke her heart. I brought the mafia into her life. I left— then I came back. She's acting like *I'm* the one who stabbed her in the back.

Technically, I am, but only metaphorically.

A grunt rumbles through my chest as I lean against the brick wall, staring across the street at Brianna's store. It's grey out today, the entire crappy city blanketed in an overcast with light drizzles of rain. My sloppy bangs stick to my forehead as I blink away droplets of water. Mist hangs thickly in the air like a humid cloak has just been draped over my shoulders. My shirt sticks to my chest, I feel the material peeling away as I push off the wall and stretch out my arms.

Today sucks. But I'm still determined to get to the bottom of things. I don't need Brianna to understand or accept all the facts, I can handle things on my end just fine. That's how I've managed to keep going all this time anyway. I was alone in prison for four years—I don't mind being alone now.

Eighteen years old with cuffs on my wrists sporting an orange jumpsuit that was two sizes too big. My first day in prison was hellish, like something from a cheap Netflix movie—worse, actually. I got the piss beaten out of me. Literally.

My cell door had been left open, letting in six guys in the middle of the night. They snatched me right out of bed and beat me like I stole something. One of them had a shank— slashed through my eyebrow, down the side of my face. I got my hand up in time to block the second slash. I can still feel the blade cutting into my palm every time I open and close my hand.

I'd screamed for help, reaching for the security guard who stood just outside the little room. He never moved. Just stood there and watched while I got my teeth kicked in and my jumpsuit torn from my body.

They left me naked and bleeding on my own floor. The guard's last words to me, "The Jägers don't run things here, little Hunter. This is Moreno territory."

Little Hunter... A nickname for members of the German mafia, the Hunters of New York. I wasn't a Hunter, but I was German. To them, that was close enough.

The guard spat on me. "Welcome to Cell Block D."

Welcome indeed.

Even though I truly hadn't been in the German mafia, I'd had no choice but to join while I was in prison. I got my head kicked in every night the first week I was in jail. At that point, it was either die or join the gang.

I did it for protection. I did it to stay alive.

Even though the prison was clearly under the control of the Spanish mafia, there were pockets of German Hunters in the facility. They took me in, shaved my head, and gave me a bullseye tattoo. The mark let everyone know that I wasn't fresh meat anymore. I'd chosen a side; if the Moreno's men touched me again, they'd have to deal with the rest of the Hunters.

That's why I got the tattoo—but not the one Brianna saw. That was one of many.

The first bullseye I got is on my back. A giant black target buzzed onto my skin. I didn't have to get it there, but I was in a dark place. I felt targeted, had always felt targeted. Even before the police took the city back, when my family was just an overlooked group of nobodies. We were too small for the head family to acknowledge us as allies, but large enough to be picked on for crappy jobs and missions.

My father would get calls in the middle of the night to clean out warehouses, move shipments of drugs, get rid of dead bodies. We were janitors to them. Not even important enough to be invited to functions that were open to the public.

I can remember the first time I attended one of the Gala Met Balls, an event held every year where the big name mafiosi would show up and donate millions of dollars to charity. It was nothing more than a way to gain brownie points with the public, remind everyone that sometimes gangsters could be kind too.

I was just ten years old when I went with my pops, he'd gotten hired to join the security team for the boss. *The* Boss. The leader of the German mafia.

Uwe Jäger.

They called him the Jägermeister, Master of Hunters.

I only ever saw him in person that one time; I was the kid who opened his door when his car pulled up to the Gala. His cologne left the vehicle before he did, a cloud of dark, wintergreen fragrance rolling out and into my nose. I can still smell his scent now, wafting around me, sending shivers up and down my spine.

His shoes had shined bright enough for me to see my own reflection, but that paled in comparison to the winking jewel he wore on his finger—the signet ring. I'd stared at it as he reached for the door handle to get out. And when he stood beside me, I pinched myself to make sure I didn't faint.

His eyes were steel grey, sharper than the dagger my father told me to keep tucked into my waistband. There was stubble along his jaw, neat and trimmed, as well-kept as the rest of him. A suit that cost more than a month of my father's wages, dark hair slicked back so I could see his face clearly. He was a handsome man, as attractive as he was scary.

I couldn't peel my eyes away, even though he'd never even looked at me. Uwe Jäger stepped from the car, adjusted his tie, and kept walking like I didn't even exist.

That was over ten years ago, when it was safe to be German in New York.

When I was eighteen, my heritage got me arrested. When I was in prison, it almost got me killed. Now, it's the reason the woman I love can't stand the sight of me.

My hands ball into fists as I replay our argument in my head. It's been on repeat since I looked into her tear-filled eyes. She doesn't want to speak unless it's to tell her what's really going on. But how can I do that? How do I convince Brianna that her father had me thrown into prison for a crime I didn't commit all just to keep me from ruining her life and his reputation?

Bri's never had a great relationship with her parents, but she will never believe they would go through those lengths just to keep her thug of a boyfriend away from her. And besides, I don't have any proof. Without evidence, I'll just sound insane. I *feel* insane. But I know I'm right.

Even if Colonel Gem didn't have anything to do with the man who robbed us and tried to rape Brianna, he *did* take advantage of the situation and had me thrown in jail. I just need confirmation—one solid bit of evidence and all this will fall apart. The truth will come out, Brianna will be safe again. And she'll finally realize I'm not the monster she thinks I am.

"If only," I mumble, leaning against the brick wall again.

I'm standing in a small alley between an overpriced boutique and a flower shop. This is the perfect spot to watch Gem Jewelers; I've got good sights of the store with enough shadows to keep me hidden from view. You'd have to walk a few steps into the alley before you'd be able to see me. That gives me a way to watch Brianna and watch my own back at the same time.

Yet, with all my precaution, with my perfect hiding spot, I see a dark car glide down the street and pull to a stop right in front of the alley I'm hiding in.

The passenger window rolls down to reveal Greyson Gem, Brianna's older brother.

I hear him let go of a dark laugh before he calls, "Robert Eckhardt."

I don't respond. Technically, that's not my name anymore—hasn't been my name since before high school. I changed it to sever ties with the mafia. Great help that did.

Greyson tries again. "I know you're there, Bobby. Come out."

I step forward from the shadows.

Greyson's still squinting when he spots me walking toward the car. "There he is! I heard you were in the area again."

I lean down to look into the window. "What do you want, Greyson?"

"To talk. Get in."

I glance up at the shop, but his sharp laughter cuts off whatever excuse I was about to offer. "Brianna won't notice if you leave. She doesn't even know you're here right now."

I sigh because he's right. I've seen Bri looking around whenever she's walking down the street, but she's never spotted me unless I wanted her to.

I open the door and slide into the passenger seat. "What is it, Grey?"

"You working again?"

"Never stopped."

He peels back into traffic and starts down the street. "But are you *working* again?"

I know what he means, but I'm not going to play this game with him. "I'm not in the mafia, Grey."

He barks out a laugh. "Not anymore, you mean."

I don't respond.

I did what I had to do to survive in prison. I joined a gang and carried my own weight—that meant taking on jobs behind bars. Moving drugs through the system, spying on rival gangsters, even taking out a few—sneaking into their cells at night, slitting throats, stabbing hearts, or just holding a pillow against their face. I did whatever was asked of me because there was never an option to say no. If I had resisted, I would've been killed. I'd seen death, had stared it in the eye my first night in prison. I wasn't going to look at it again.

I thought all the violence would end when I was released, and in a way, it did. But ever since I got out, I've been met with a new challenge. Greyson Gem.

He's been the thorn in my side since I walked out of the penitentiary. For the two years that I was with Brianna, Colonel

Gem was my nightmare, but he lost interest in me after I got out. I spent a year bouncing around Jersey, hopping from job to job. Money brought me back to New York, but not *dirty* money.

I caught wind of a private security company that was willing to hire former convicts; word around the block was they were run by former mafia. Stronghold Inc. was the name; I looked them up, sent in an application, and waited for a call. They hired me within a week.

I was grateful to work for the Stronghold, but taking the job meant moving back to New York. I tried to get assignments out of town, lay low so no one would realize I was back in the city. Then I heard about Brianna's attack, and that changed everything.

"You keeping tabs on me?" I ask Greyson.

"I sniffed you out the minute you entered the Lincoln Tunnel." Grey laughs so hard he snorts. "I didn't care enough to reach out when you first came back. As far as I was concerned, you weren't a threat."

"And now what am I?"

"That depends."

I look at him and startle when I realize his eyes are right on me—not on the road, not on the steering wheel or on the scenery passing by. Greyson Gem has his brown eyes focused entirely on my face, like he's searching me for something.

After a moment, he finds what he's looking for because he returns his gaze to the street and nods.

"Depends on what?" I try to gage him.

"You're working for my sister."

"I am."

"Is it just work?"

"Greyson—"

"You trying to get laid, Bobby?"

I give him a flat face. "No, Grey, I'm not."

"Good." He laughs. "'Cause whatever happened in high school is in the past, Bobby boy. All that lovey dovey crap is long gone." He looks at me again, this time his eyes are dark but his mouth is still smiling—it's vulpine and evil. "You hear me, boy?"

Greyson is eight years older than me. I've always respected him as Bri's older brother, but he's not about to call me *boy* and get away with it.

"Don't call me that," I grind out.

He slaps my shoulder, momentarily disarming me. "Calm your milkers."

My milkers...

I blink at him. "Just take me back to the store."

"Not until I'm satisfied."

"Satisfied with what?"

"With your answers to my questions."

"Everyone's got questions," I mumble.

"Do they?"

His words draw my attention. I shift in my seat to find him quirking an eyebrow at me. It's thick and raven-colored, standing out starkly against his brown skin. Greyson's lighter than his sister, his tone more of a caramel compared to

Brianna's chocolate brown. He's got the same coiled hair as her, though he keeps his short and weighed down by product. Bri mostly wears hers in an angry, untamable afro. In high school, she would get in trouble for wearing it naturally. Our teachers were constantly complaining that it wasn't neat enough, according to their standards.

Oh ... the struggles of Black hair.

"Who else has questions?" Greyson asks.

"No one," I mutter.

"Good." He taps the steering wheel with his thumb. "No one has questions because you don't have answers. Got it?"

"You don't own me, Grey."

"Yes, I do." The words roll off his tongue so casually I almost nod agreement, but I catch myself and glare at him instead. He speaks before I can produce any words. "You want another four years?"

My breath hitches. Aside from Colonel's threat on the day of my release, this is the closest I've ever come to getting a confession out of these people.

"What will you tell Brianna this time if I'm arrested again?"

"That you're still a scumbag. Came back to hit it, realized you couldn't, so you dipped. Again."

I want to punch him, but Greyson's likely to have me tossed in prison for it. The Gems are richer than when I left and good old Uncle Lee is now *Commissioner* Lee. They have more resources and more power—everything they need for Grey to do exactly what he wants with me.

I have to be careful.

"I'm just doing my job. I have a contract," I say slowly. "It's all legal—"

"Calm down." He waves a hand like hanging a four-year prison sentence over my head is nothing to panic about. "I'm glad you're Bri's security guard."

"You are?"

"Of course." He turns the corner smoothly, and I glance out the window, realizing we're back at the store. "You'll keep Brianna in line for me."

"In line with what?"

Greyson pulls over to my alley. "With my rules."

"You want me to control her."

"I want you to watch her. Exactly what you've been doing. Just give me updates."

"Greyson—"

"Four years is a long time, Bobby boy."

I grind my teeth, sanding my hands together to keep from wrapping them around Greyson's throat. He won't get to hold this over my head forever.

Greyson slaps my shoulder and unlocks the car doors. "I'll call on you in the future."

Like a child who's just been dismissed, I step out the car and into the rain, slinking back into the shadows without a word.

9

Bobby is lying on my couch when I leave my bedroom this morning. Normally, I would get angry and toss him out, but he looks so peaceful, it feels wrong to interrupt his nap.

I have no idea what Bobby does all day—I mean, I know he guards me, but he never eats unless I force him to and he doesn't sleep as far as I can tell. If I stay out until 4 a.m. then Bobby stays out until 4 a.m. and he's waiting outside my door the next morning by the time I'm ready to leave. I know it's his job to stay ready 24/7, I know I'm paying him for every second of his time, but he's still human. He still needs to eat, still needs a moment to relax, and if his presence on my couch is anything to learn from, he apparently still needs to sleep.

He's lying on his back, an arm slung over his eyes as he rests. Bobby's so tall he takes up almost the entire couch, his feet dangerously close to hanging off the end. I can hear his soft breathing, like the snores of a child, his chest rising and falling with each deep breath. He must have come in late last night when he was sure I'd be asleep and wouldn't hear him settling in for the night.

Absently, I wonder how many nights he's secretly spent on my couch, sleeping right in my living room and leaving before I wake up for work. I could chew him out for coming when we'd agreed to have no contact, but as soon as I open my mouth to wake him, his eyes peel open, and I'm frozen by his icy blue stare.

He blinks tiredly and then smiles. Rubs at his eyes. "Morning, Princess."

I don't know what to say, partly because I'm embarrassed that he caught me staring, but also because we haven't spoken in days. Not since I yelled at him on the street and told him he wasn't anything more than hired help. The fact that Bobby can still smile and greet me in the morning after being the victim of my rage almost yanks an apology from my throat.

I swallow and give him a firm nod, one downward jerk of my chin. "Morning."

He rolls onto his side, resting his chin on his fist. "You caught me sleeping."

"Late night?"

He nods. "Had to check in with my boss after you got home. Took longer than I thought so I crashed here instead of sleeping at my place and coming back."

"And where exactly is your place?" I turn and start walking toward the open kitchen. Even though we've been keeping our distance, Bobby's still made it a point to restock my fridge once a week. I think it's more for the convenience of being able to fix himself a sandwich whenever he wants rather than caring about my starved cupboards, but whatever.

"I live in Brooklyn," he tells me.

I hope he doesn't see me stiffen across the room. Brooklyn is German territory. The mafia's been gone for ten years now, but there are still smalltime criminals who guard the streets like dark patrolmen. That's how I got stabbed back in high school, went down the wrong alley on the wrong night in Queens.

I don't want to venture into our past, so I stay quiet as I make two cups of coffee. When I turn to pass Bobby a mug, he takes it without a word and sips in silence. This is the first time we've spoken since that horrible argument almost a week ago. It feels good to get along with him, at least in some way, but I still haven't worked through my emotions. I still haven't gotten over the blank spaces in our past. He has all the information to clear the air, but he's convinced I can't handle it. His assumptions make me burn with anger, but, secretly, I think he might be right.

Since the argument, I've been popping my meds like they're candy. Each pill summons tears and muttered prayers as I wallow in guilt. I feel like I'm unraveling and there's no one who can put me back together. My mother would never understand, her judgmental church friends would never understand, Bobby wouldn't even understand.

At night, it's just me and God but I feel like He's not listening. Or maybe my mother is right. Maybe the meds cloud my head, and I can't hear whether He's speaking or not.

I sigh away my frustration as I look up at Bobby. He's watching me over the rim of his mug. "I'm ready to leave for work," I mumble, turning toward the door.

He leaves behind me without a word.

Like usual, Bobby slips into the Manhattan crowd and disappears as soon as we exit my apartment building. I'm used to him doing that now, but I can't stop myself from glancing around in search of him. It's like trying to find my own shadow, something that's always with you but *just* out of reach.

When I get inside the store, Lyla is already there setting up. The diamonds have been polished and the display boxes have all been shined. The place looks good, but before I can tell this to my assistant, she squeals and runs over to me with an envelope in her hand.

Lyla crushes me in a hug and then pulls back to hop up and down. "Ms. Gem! You're finally here!"

It's 7:30 in the morning, the usual time I'm here.

"Happy to see me?" I ask warily.

She gasps and thrusts the envelope at me. "This came early!"

I take it and pull out the card inside. Just by the creamy feel of the thick paper, I can tell it's an expensive note. Then I spot the T.D.I. insignia at the bottom of the page and I gasp in excitement.

T.D.I. stands for The Diamond Industry, an elite magazine that showcases the world's best stones. They only have two issues a year, ranking the new cuts, designs, and the stores which sell them. Once a year, they hold a convention for stores featured in their issues to display their best jewels. As a nod to the new guys on the block, they also invite some of the smaller or recently opened stores.

At least two of my father's stores have been featured in every issue of The Diamond Industry's magazine for the last eight years. Greyson got his first feature last year with the pink diamond display he set up in his first store. Both of them had a table at T.D.I.'s convention.

This year, I'll get a table too.

I wasn't featured in their recent issue, but T.D.I. has invited me to hold a display at their upcoming convention. The joy that screams through me escapes my mouth in a cry of victory. I'm in tears before I know it, hugging Lyla and jumping up and down with her like two little girls.

"I can't believe this!" I scream.

"You did it!" she screams back.

"God did it," I correct her. I have no idea what Lyla's beliefs are, but I'm not going to take the Lord's credit for myself. I know for a fact I didn't earn this invitation, not with my store in danger of closing and our displays nearly two years out of style.

This invitation is a pity invite, considering the convention is less than three weeks away and I have virtually zero time to prepare. Grey got his invite almost eight months ago, giving him enough time to secure those pretty chocolate diamonds.

I'm not fooled by the expensive letter and the fancy cursive writing. I know I've only been invited because I'm the daughter of the Gem Legend himself. T.D.I. will benefit from my presence at the convention, whether I deserve to be there or not. There'll be three Gem displays in the same place at the same time—we might even outsell Jäger Diamonds altogether.

I have no doubts T.D.I. invited me just to stir up buzz and competition, but I'm happy, nonetheless. This is a huge opportunity for the store. The convention will host a charity ball and allow the upper crusts of New York to bid on the jewels sparkling around them. It's a chance to walk away with over a hundred million bucks, even with the portion of proceeds that'll go to charity. For whatever reason, rich people don't want to pay 75 thousand for a nice diamond in the store, but they'll bid 4 million on that same diamond for charity. I'm not complaining, especially since the stores which sell diamonds to bidders get to keep 50 percent of the bid.

I'm so excited, I call almost everyone I know. Greyson congratulates me dryly and then says he's got a client waiting, my father rumbles his compliments over the phone and tells me he's proud of me, my mother screams and says we need to meet for lunch. I don't really want to suffer another lunch with her, but I figure she'll be willing to play nice since she's happy for me. I tell her I'll pencil her in tomorrow and then I spend the rest of my morning making preparations.

I don't have a fancy new set of diamonds like Greyson. I don't have a reputation like the Colonel's. But I do have Gem as my last name, and I've got enough prayers to fill up two request boxes at church.

Lyla and I both grit our teeth and knock our heads together as we go through our contacts, trying to call in every favor we can. I'm looking to build a beautiful set for my display with a 'Fire & Ice' theme for the jewels. Only thing is, I don't have fire and ice jewels.

Red, blue, and orange diamonds would work perfectly for this display but the stones we have are mediocre at best. I'm going to look like a mall franchise rather than the million-dollar boutique I want to be. I grew up in a family of billionaires and this is the best I can do.

I sigh in defeat as I hang up the phone in my office. I'd called almost everyone on my list of contacts, and no one had given me a chance. Lyla managed to convince a celebrity we sold a diamond necklace to last year to give the jewelry back for a hefty compensation. People will definitely want to bid on a necklace that'd once been worn by a movie star, which means we'll be able to make back the money I've shed to reacquire the jewelry. But we need more than one necklace and we've only got three weeks to secure everything, plus build the set we'll use for our display.

My father and brother have been planning for almost a year—Grey's chocolate diamonds will be on a dessert themed display called 'Edible Rocks.' My father's display will feature an array of green and true orange diamonds in a setting he's named simply, 'Autumn.'

Nearly all the joy I'd had this morning is gone by the time lunch rolls around. I'm suddenly glad I decided not to go out with my mother until tomorrow. I know she'll have a hundred questions and I've just realized I've got no answers.

We have one diamond and a nice display idea. Nothing more.

Bobby notices my sour mood when he slides into the chair

across from me at the diner I picked for lunch. As shocked as I am to see him in the flesh and not hiding in the street somewhere, I have to say, I'd been looking forward to enjoying my food alone today.

"You picked a bad time to come out of the shadows," I say solemnly.

Bobby drags my untouched roast beef across the table and starts eating. "You've been wearing that defeated look since you sat down. Thought I could cheer you up."

This would be an opportune moment to start asking questions, but I know I'm not in the right mindset for whatever answers he's got. Right now, I just want to focus on happy things. By the grace of God, I've been invited to The Diamond Industry Convention. Despite my small setbacks, I have a lot to be excited over. I want answers, but not at the cost of this rare moment of joy.

I just want to enjoy this, I say inside.

"What's on your mind?" Bobby asks, adding salt to the gravy on his beef. He sops up the brown liquid with a roll and then stuffs the whole thing into his mouth.

"Gem Jewelers got invited to The Diamond Industry Convention this year."

Bobby frowns. "That's in, like, three weeks."

"I know."

"Now I see why you're stressed."

It's been six years, but Bobby remembers all the planning and work that went into my father's displays each year when one of his stores got invited. Our junior year of high school, my father trusted us enough to work the display ourselves, wearing matching uniforms and trying our best to sound professional as we described the diamonds to interested bidders.

Now, I'm setting up my own display and Bobby is here to help once again, if only as my private security. The nostalgia is insane, bringing a crooked smile to my face, but it's wiped away by Bobby's next words.

"You shouldn't go."

I stare at him. "Are you kidding?"

"No."

"Bobby—"

"You got attacked two months ago, and you were almost attacked again a few weeks ago when you hired me."

"What's that got to do with anything?"

He pushes the plate away and tents his fingers on the table. "Don't you think maybe this invitation could be a trap of some sort?"

I almost laugh at him. "Seriously? I got jumped by a random thug—"

"You don't know that for certain."

My eyes narrow. "Do *you* know anything for certain?"

He sighs. "I'm just saying."

"So am I. I'm not being targeted by secret assassins trying to lure me out. If that's the case, they could have gotten to me at any point in the two months I was alone before hiring you."

For a long moment, Bobby doesn't speak. He just sits there staring at me, his jaw clenched tightly, his eyes sharpened to a point. I want to squirm beneath his dangerous gaze, but I steel myself and lift my chin. If he thinks he can scare me with his vague suggestions of danger, he's got another thing coming.

This invitation is an opportunity from God. I need this more than he will ever know because Bobby will be gone when his contract is up, but I'll still be here with my struggling store. I'm going to the convention no matter what.

"I know there's a lot you haven't told me about what happened six years ago. But I can't let my fears of the past stop me from chasing what's right in front of me."

He exhales slowly, flared nostrils betraying his calm voice. "I just want you to be safe."

"Then keep me safe."

"I will," he says seriously. "I'd take a bullet for you, Bri. But I'm not going to let you walk right into danger."

"What makes you think I'll be in danger at the convention?"

"It just doesn't make sense."

My eyebrows lower. "What doesn't make sense?" When he doesn't speak, I fold my arms and glare at him. "What doesn't make sense, Bobby?"

I want to hear him say it.

"The fact that I got invited, right? You can't believe I managed to find some sort of success. That means it *must* be a setup. The *only* reason I could ever score an invitation to T.D.I. is if someone wants to lure me out and kill me."

He starts to shake his head. "It's not a matter of your success—"

"Why can't you just be happy for me?"

"I am happy for you." He leans across the table and his hand extends toward me but stops short, like he's just remembered not to touch me. The sad thing is, I want him to touch me. I need a reassuring hand, a kind gesture. But coming from Bobby, I know it would mean more than it should.

We sit in silence for an awkward moment.

Bobby clears his throat. "I'm tired of fighting, Bri."

I am too.

I sigh. "You should go."

Bobby looks defeated, but only for a moment. The emotion that flickers over his face is gone as soon as he blinks. By the time he stands, he's wearing that indifferent mask I've seen him wear so many times. It isn't a face he's worn just while working with me, it's an expression he mastered long ago, when we were still in school.

Bobby could be a hothead at times, but he didn't *like* fighting. Didn't *like* putting up with the jerks who teased him every day. Sometimes he would say something back, sometimes he would stand up for himself. But when he got tired, when he just gave up, he wouldn't react at all. Not when students called him poor, not when teachers singled him out for his possible connection to the mafia, not even when my parents would say he wasn't good enough for me.

Instead of getting angry and lashing out, Bobby would keep a cool face, like the comments never bothered him. He's wearing that face now, except I can see right through it. He really is worried about me, whether it's unfounded or not isn't the point. Something's got Bobby spooked enough that he truly believes I could be in danger by going to this convention.

I reach for him as he walks past me. It's enough to stop him in his tracks, cracking the mask he's secured to his face. Bobby looks down at me in complete shock, blinking at the hand I've placed over his.

"I'm not going to pass up this opportunity," I say softly. "But I do appreciate you worrying about me."

He nods, and I feel his long fingers curl around mine as he says, "Just be careful, Bri."

10

My sofa is empty when I emerge from my bedroom this morning. I'm not surprised since Bobby was only taking a nap the last time it happened, but I am surprised when I open my front door and he isn't waiting for me to leave. Any other day, I'd assume he was already waiting in the lobby or on the street like he does sometimes, but today I know he's nowhere to be found.

There's a giant man standing outside my door instead of the gorgeous blonde I hired. He's a monster of a man—taller than Bobby and twice as bulky. His face is a collection of scars with a grimacing mouth in the center; you could almost miss his mouth if you weren't looking directly at it. His black beard is so thick and bushy, I'm positive he's lost things in there before.

Our eyes lock when I close my door behind me and step forward. Even though he's big, the man isn't particularly intimidating, just scary to look at for more than a few seconds.

"Uh," I say slowly.

He holds out his hand, when I take it, I feel like I'm gripping a baseball mitt—it's just as big and leathery. "Hans Vogt," he says, and his accent is so strong it takes me an extra moment to realize he's introduced himself.

Like an idiot, I say the first thing that pops into my head. "You're German."

Hans's thick eyebrows lower a fraction. "Yes. Is that a problem?"

"No. It's just…" I sigh. "Where's Bobby?"

"He sent me in his place."

"Why?"

"He's been called away."

I turn away before Hans can see the frown that dashes over my face. I don't want to believe it, but part of me wonders if our argument yesterday has anything to do with Bobby's sudden disappearance. It's not like he'd tell that to Hans anyway, so there's no point in wondering. Besides, I've got way too much on my mind to think about Bobby and his mood swings. If he wants to bounce on the job after one small disagreement, then that's him.

He won't be missed.

I *almost* miss Bobby when Hans follows me to work. He is nothing like my blonde shadow, melting into the crowd to become invisible at a moment's notice. Hans walks right beside me like an actual security guard, his massive form scaring innocent bystanders. I mean, technically, he's doing his job right, I'm just not used to such a forward style. Where Bobby likes to watch from the shadows and take action only when necessary, Hans likes to frighten everyone from the get-go and dare them to try something.

I make it to the store alive, so I guess I can't complain.

Lyla stares at Hans when he enters Gem Jewelers behind me; she knows about Bobby being my security, but she doesn't know about him being my ex or all the fighting we've been doing. I can see all the questions swirling in her head as she enters my office and slowly closes the door behind her.

"Where did Brad Pitt go?" she asks with a wrinkle in her dark eyebrows. She's got pretty black hair but always keeps it hidden beneath a wig. I've seen Lyla as a blonde, brunette, and one time she wore a green and white wig for St. Patrick's Day. This month, she installed a red lace front, it's straight and sleek and looks good against her light brown skin.

I sigh at Bobby's nickname. "He got called away."

"For how long?"

I pause. *How long* hadn't occurred to me yet, but I don't want Lyla to know that I'm in the dark, so I give her my sternest look and my most serious boss-like voice. "He'll be back before the convention."

That seems to satisfy her as she nods and turns to leave. I huff out a sigh and resolve to spend as much time in the main lobby as possible. Hans has taken up a corner in the front of the store, I don't want to watch him grimace at my customers all day, but I also don't *want* him to grimace at them all day, so I pull on my big girl panties and get ready to do my job.

We manage to make a few sales today; I think it's because we hung a little banner outside the door announcing our invitation to the T.D.I. Convention—it came with the letter. People are curious to see a sample of what's going to be up for grabs at the fancy little ball. Some of the snobbier customers walk away with wrinkled noses, but most people are nice and some even coughed up impressive down payments for the orders we collected. That'll give me the credit I need to start building the set for my display.

Speaking of which, I decide to skip my lunch and head to the convention center to check out my staging area. I get to wear a neat little badge and everything—it feels like VIP treatment, and even though I grew up in a family of billionaire jewelers, I can't stop myself from grinning like a kid as I walk around the event space.

Most of the place is empty, but there are some areas that have been roped off with the frames of display sets resting in the center. Everything I see is just bare bones, but I'm excited, inspired, and impressed, nonetheless.

My area is pathetically small, squeezed between the wall and the massive space cleared for Grey's setup. T.D.I. decided to clump the three Gem stores together with a nice area for us to share, but it's clear I'm the runt of the pack because the set portioned out for Gem Jewelers isn't even a third of the size of Grey's, not to mention the area cleared for my father's set.

No worries. Little do they know, I can't afford a large set anyway, so the joke's on them.

I spend an hour just staring at the roped area, imagining

my Fire & Ice setup glowing and shining in the center. I want to build a miniature waterfall that pours over an ice sculpture glowing from an orange backlight. It'll be a hefty project, and it'll cost a fortune to get it done in time, but I know it'll be beautiful. Imagine the diamonds set over the ice, winking as they're gently sprayed by the mist of the waterfall.

When my fancy dreams fade back to reality, I sit on the floor and pull out my laptop. The next three hours pass in a daze as I send emails and make phone calls right there on the floor of the convention center. I don't have to sit on the concrete and work, but I want to keep my empty space—my goal—right in front of me.

As I work, everything around me seems to melt away. My anxiety, my worries over Bobby's disappearance, even Hans's annoying presence doesn't bother me as I type away at my keyboard. The only thing that truly disrupts me is the chime of my watch as an alarm buzzes for me to take my medicine.

I shut it off and decide to take a dose of Scripture instead. Verna's text is still saved in my phone; I scroll through the Bible verses she sent and then lie on my back. "God... I need Your help," I whisper. It isn't a desperate prayer like the ones I usually scream-cry at night (into my pillow so Bobby won't hear). This prayer feels natural, genuine. Like I'm talking to someone who's in the room with me, and I know He's listening.

My phone buzzes again, this time it isn't an alarm, it's a call from my mother.

All at once, I remember we had plans for lunch and I jerk

upright with a gasp. "Crap!"

"Is that a way to speak to your mother?" Mama says as I answer the phone.

I slap my forehead. "Sorry. I didn't realize I'd answered."

"So, you meant to ignore my call?"

"No—Mom, I, uh…" She breathes into the phone so loudly I'm not sure if she's okay for a second. "I'm sorry," I mutter, standing from the floor and brushing out the skirt of my dress. I gather my laptop as she scolds me for forgetting about our plans, then I make promises to meet her right now as I practically sprint out of the convention center. To my shock, Hans is hot on my heels, running like he's in a Mission Impossible movie. I don't even know how to react to that, so I just keep moving until I make it outside and hail a cab.

"I'll meet you at my place in an hour," I tell my mother. "I'll even cook dinner myself." With all the groceries Bobby's been buying, I know I've got ingredients to whip up something.

Mom begrudgingly agrees to allow me to cook food for her with my peasant self, then she smooches the phone and hangs up.

I sigh as I sit back in the seats, more than aware of Hans's presence beside me in the cab. He's so big, I'm nearly squished against the passenger door with his big knee pressed against my own.

"Your other clients ever complain about your size?" I ask him.

He laughs heartily. "My other clients usually hire me for

different jobs."

I press my lips together, wondering if he's lowkey confessing to being a hitman. As I sneak a glance at him, I catch sight of the bullseye tattooed onto the palm of his right hand.

"Are you from the Hunting Grounds?" I ask in a whisper.

Hans turns to look at me dead-on. "I was a member before it fell. Worked with the Jägermeister himself, and his oldest son."

I swallow. "Is that how you know Bobby?"

He frowns. It's so ugly. "I know Robert from work. We're both security guards for Stronghold Inc. Nothing more."

"I see."

The car falls silent, though the tension in the air makes me feel like screaming. I see the cab driver looking at me through the rearview mirror, when our eyes meet, he glances away and focuses on the road again.

"I didn't mean to imply anything," I say, feeling like I need to explain myself.

Hans grunts, it's a rumble so deep and loud, I would have guessed the driver had revved his engine. "I am not insulted by your curiosity. I know who I used to be—I am still that person, just changed careers. Not even by choice."

This man basically said he was a killer before and is still a killer now. Just not on paper. Retired, I suppose.

I make the sign of the Cross as *discreetly* as I can and then look over at Hans. He's staring at me with his little eyes all squinted. I squint back, trying to find his mouth. When his beard wiggles, I realize he's smiling at me. He should really shave that thing.

"Go ahead and ask what you really want to know," Hans orders.

I squirm in my seat. I'd love to ask about Bobby, get info on what he's been doing at Stronghold Inc., find out if he was ever in the Hunting Grounds with Hans, but I keep my mouth shut.

First of all, Hans is an old man. He's at least fifty with his salt and pepper sideburns and suspiciously black beard. I won't assume he dyes it, but... With him being so much older than Bobby, I doubt he would know much about him in the Hunting Grounds.

The mafia ruled New York City uncontested for ten years. Their rise to power started with the killing of a citizen during a routine arrest with police. There were rumors the incident was racially motivated which sparked public outcry to defund the police. New York gave in and slashed finances for their department, forcing them to lay off over half their forces. This paved the way for the gangs of New York to completely take over the city.

The Big Apple spent ten years gripped in anarchy before the police managed to take the city back. I was four years old when the defunding happened, fourteen when the police rescued New York, and now I'm twenty-four—same age as Bobby.

That means my rebellious ex was too young to be involved in the German mafia during its hay day. There were still pockets of the mafia left behind when law enforcement rolled in, skirmishes and shootouts with police were common the first few years after the gangs fell. But Bobby and I were only kids then. Even if the rumors about his family were true, I don't think Bobby himself played a role in the mafia when we were together.

Now, though.

Now, Bobby's got multiple bullseyes tattooed all over his body. He's been MIA for the last six years and he works for a private security company that seems to specialize in hiring former gangsters. Plus, all the murky water surrounding my first attack when we were teens.

I have so many questions. But I won't ask Hans anything. It's not my place.

Whatever Bobby's been up to, whatever secrets he's got to share about his past, I want to hear it from him. He would never forgive me for snooping around behind his back, asking questions to his coworkers. And from the way Hans is creepily grinning at me, I doubt I'd get many answers anyway. He strikes me as the type to lead you to the edge and laugh while you teeter.

When we get to my apartment, my mother is waiting in the lobby with two of her church friends. They're being entertained by the handsome bellhop who's smiling and flashing his dimples as he delivers a joke which they find hilarious. I'm grateful for his presence because it distracts my mother from my very late arrival—and gives me the time to greet my cousin Verna who's decided to tag along with my mom.

"We were at Bible study," she whispers to me as we hug. "Thought I'd come over to help out with dinner."

"Thank you," I whisper back.

When I pull away, I find my mother sitting with her two friends, Mr. and Mrs. Barker. They're old people I've seen at church more times than I can remember, but I'm not particularly happy to see them now. Mr. and Mrs. Barker are generally kind, but right now they're just more mouths to feed. Thankfully, Verna's here to help.

We make it to my apartment in a cluster, everyone waits outside the door as I nervously unlock it. I can feel their eyes shifting between me and Hans but we both ignore them and move inside without a word. Hans takes up space by the door while my mother and her two friends drift to the living room. I pass Verna a pitcher of lemonade from the fridge to serve them while I dash to my bedroom and swap my beige business dress for a pair of comfortable jeans and an oversized flannel.

I smell food cooking when I come out, and a smile immediately lights up my face. Verna's at the stove with a spoon in her hand, hovered over a pan of gravy.

"What's for dinner?" I ask, sniffing at the pan.

She smiles as I kiss her cheek. "Smothered porkchops and mashed potatoes with roasted veggies for my little cousin."

I grin. Verna's always been a better cook than me, I'm looking forward to dinner.

She glances at me and then nods her head in Hans's

direction. "You finally settled on a guard?"

"Uh, he's my backup guard," I admit.

"Who was the first guard?"

I take a deep breath. "Bobby Ackard."

Verna's spoon stops, but it's my mother who speaks up. I hadn't even noticed her approach the counter, empty lemonade glasses in hand. She's staring at me with a look on her face that's somehow crossed between confusion, shock, and anger.

"Bobby Ackard?" she whispers.

"Mom—"

She shakes her head and sets down the glasses with more force than necessary. "How dare you bring that miscreant back into our lives."

"He's changed," I say quickly. My words shock both of us. I can't believe I'm defending Bobby, but my mother is shocked for a different reason.

"He got you stabbed." She frowns. "After all these years, you're still in love with that lowlife."

My eyebrows go so far up my head I'm scared for my hairline. "I'm not in love with Bobby!" I almost yell. Over my mother's shoulder, I can see Mr. and Mrs. Barker glancing over with nervous looks on their faces.

"Lower your voice!" my mother orders. "You will not speak to me that way, especially not in front of my friends from church."

"What difference does it make where they're from?" I say nastily.

My mother's face curdles in anger. "Of course you don't care about church." She tosses up her hands. "Look at what you've done with your life. It shows how much you don't care."

I clench my jaw to keep from snapping at her.

This is so unfair. I know I've messed up—a lot. I had sex before marriage, with a boy my parents had warned me about time and again. I started smoking in high school. I used wine and meds as my counselors instead of seeking *The* Counselor. But I'm sorry and I'm trying to make things better.

No one cares that I poured the wine down the sink. No one cares that I've been trying to cut back on the meds. No one cares that I've been working to forgive Bobby for everything he's done. Nope. The only thing my mother sees when she looks at me is my mistakes.

It's the same for the *clean and wholesome* church folk on my sofa right now. I can see the judgment in their eyes as my mother rants about how messed up I am, and how much I've disappointed her. Nothing she says is new. Dear old Mom has hissed my business around the congregation since I was a teenager sneaking off with my trailer trash boyfriend.

That mafia White boy is what Mama used to call him. Can you believe such a warm and welcoming woman of God would say such a thing?

I can.

It's all I've ever heard from her and her so-called church friends. Judgement.

I know not every Christian is like this but, lately, this sort

113

of treatment is all I've been faced with. If it weren't for Verna and her unconditional love and kindness, I would've given up on my faith long ago.

What hurts the most is that this attitude comes from the very people who are supposed to love and support me. What a joke. The same people who invite me to church are the ones who point their fingers and shake their heads *every single time* I make a mistake.

My anger builds as I try to block out my mother's words. Sweet Verna senses my rage boiling and steps over to diffuse the situation. "Aunt Shelly—"

"No, Verna," my mother says sharply. "Brianna needs to hear this."

"I've heard it for the last six years," I say slowly. "I'm done hearing it."

She blinks rapidly. "Who do you think you're talking to?"

"I need you to leave." My voice cracks as I speak, and I feel a lump form in my throat. I swallow it down and swipe at the tear slipping down my cheek. "Please leave," I repeat.

My mother just stands there, stunned and offended. "How dare you," is the only thing she says to me before gathering her things and her friends and marching out the door.

As soon as it clicks shut, I break down in tears.

11

Verna wraps me in her arms almost immediately. "It's okay," she whispers, petting the back of my head. She moves me to the sofa and sits me down, taking a seat beside me so she can clutch my hands and look me in the eye.

"Don't let them get to you," she says, squeezing my hands.

"How can I not? She's my *mother*."

She winces, and even though Verna's relationship with her own mother has been nothing but pleasant, I know she understands what I'm saying. The words mean so much more coming from the woman who raised you.

"How can they be so cruel?" I whisper. "All they do is judge me. I can't stand it."

"Mr. And Mrs. Barker are innocent," Verna says.

I shake my head, pulling my hands from hers. "No one is innocent. Anyone my mother hands around is just another gossip buddy. They all look at me the same way, like they're ashamed to be around me."

"I'm not ashamed."

I managed a wobbly smile. "Because you're a real Christian. A true Believer."

She is. Verna's the only one who's never judged me for my mistakes, never brought them up or threw them in my face whenever she got angry. And she's never treated my hiccups as late-night gossip, sharing all the dirty details with her friends.

Instead of pointing her finger, Verna's always offered her hands in prayer. Instead of hissing insults, she's sent me scriptures and encouraging words. Instead of reminding me of my mistakes, she's always reminded me that I'm still a child of the Most High God, no matter what I've done.

She reaches for her purse on the coffee table and fishes out her phone. I know she's got her Bible app pulled up when she starts reading a scripture.

"One who has unreliable friends soon comes to ruin, but there is a friend who sticks closer than a brother."

I wipe at my nose. "Proverbs eighteen, verse twenty-four."

She nods. "Jesus is still here with you, Bri. And He's on your side, even when your own family is against you."

"I just don't understand why she treats me like this. Why *anyone* treats me like this. As if they haven't made mistakes."

"We're human," Verna says simply. "We are our own worst enemy sometimes."

"Now I sincerely understand why people leave the Church."

She sighs. "You can't let the mistakes of Christians stop you from following Christ. Every time you let their behavior get to you, the devil wins." She leans forward, her brows flattening as she says seriously, "Don't let him win, Bri. Keep pushing."

I want to throw in the towel. Grab my meds, a bottle of wine, and pass out with some horrible Netflix movie playing in the background. But I know Verna's right. I can't give up on God just because some people who call themselves Christians hurt my feelings.

Verna's smile is gentle, almost cautious. "The Book of Romans says, *rejoice with those who rejoice; mourn with those who mourn*." She laughs lightly. "It's easy to join in with celebration, but sometimes we forget to mourn with those who mourn. Because we've forgotten what it's like to mourn, we've forgotten the pain we experienced during our own trials and tribulations." Verna pats my hand. "And when you forget your own pain, it's difficult to sympathize with someone else's. That makes it tough to be kind—to *treat others the way you want to be treated*."

I roll my eyes. "I haven't met a single Christian who's treated people the way they want to be treated. Myself included." That last statement is mumbled under my breath as an image of Bobby pops into my head.

I'm suddenly reminded of how horrible I've treated him since he showed up for an interview weeks ago. I yelled at him, didn't give him the chance to speak, accused him of being in a gang, and reminded him of his crimes against me every chance I got.

I've treated him exactly the way my mother has been treating me.

117

Fresh tears fill my eyes. "I'm just as much a monster as my mom."

Verna blinks at me, confused by the sudden confession. "No, you're not," she argues.

"I am!" I exclaim, which makes me seem crazy because I'm yelling and crying and Verna has no idea why. She doesn't know anything about what's happened between me and Bobby these last few weeks—she hadn't even known he was my security guard until twenty minutes ago.

Nevertheless, sweet Verna rubs my back until my tears begin to slow, then she says calmly, "You need to pray about these things, Bri. Your problems aren't going to magically go away one day. Hand them over to God."

"I know." I sigh. "I do pray. Sometimes. I should pray more often." I shrug sheepishly. "Sometimes I just wish I had a person to talk to." I hate saying that because it feels like I'm telling Verna that God isn't enough. He *is*—He's more than enough. But my relationship with God is weak... I can admit that. I don't feel the security that someone like Verna feels.

When I pray, I get silence in return. I know God hears. But my faith isn't strong enough to hear His reply. Not yet at least.

Verna reaches for her purse again and pulls out a pamphlet. "Have you tried counseling?"

"Verna, they already hate me for the meds. What will everyone think of a Christian going to therapy?"

She passes me the paper. "I interned at this clinic during my last semester of undergrad."

Verna has a bachelor's in psychology, and she's been

118

working toward her master's the last eight months. She's gotten a lot of slack for it, since most of the Church still believes psychology is from the devil, but I'm proud of her accomplishments.

I glance down at the pamphlet she's given me, bold gold lettering stares back at me. **Crown Clinic**. The name sounds interesting, along with the thorny crown logo they have. There's also a big cross in the background, behind the information listing their hours and the names of the doctors who work there.

Verna says, "This is a Christian clinic. Every psychologist there is a Believer. Appointments are just one hour long, and they're focused on strengthening your relationship with Christ, pointing you back to Him during your troubles, not offering man-made solutions." She beams. "Their meetings feel more like one-hour prayer sessions, to be honest."

"You've gone?" I ask.

She nods. "Earning my master's has been more stressful than I thought it would be. With the size of our church, I can't get one-on-one sessions with Pastor Amber Jones. Therapy is as good as it gets. Of course, I spend a lot of time in prayer too, but seeing Dr. Jensen has helped build my trust in God. After a few months, I realized I needed the sessions less and less. Now I'm confident taking my issues directly to the Lord. I don't need an in-between to help me." She squeezes my shoulder. "But there's nothing wrong with those who do."

"I don't know," I say slowly.

Verna scrolls through her Bible app again. "*Accept the one whose faith is weak, without quarreling over disputable matters.*" She looks up at me. "Romans fourteen and one. Do you know what that means?"

Uh...

"Not really."

"It means that sometimes Christians face issues that can seem a little tricky to solve. Is it okay for Believers to go to therapy? To take medication for anxiety or depression? In these sorts of circumstances, we often determine what's right or wrong based on what we *personally* approve of. Not on what God approves of."

I nod. "Sounds about right."

"Verse twenty-two pretty much sums this up—*so whatever you believe about these things keep between yourself and God. Blessed is the one who does not condemn himself by what he approves.*" She presses her lips together disappointedly. "We don't always agree on the same things; those of weaker faith may lean toward counseling while those of greater faith are bold enough to go straight to the Throne of Grace. There's nothing wrong with either one. The point of this scripture is that those of greater faith mustn't judge those of weaker faith. We must accept them *without quarrelling.*"

"You need to tell this to my mother and her church friends," I say with a laugh, trying to lighten the air.

Verna smirks. "There are people all over the world like you, Brianna. People who have been judged and ostracized by their own brothers and sisters in Christ. Dr. Jensen and her team make it a point to create a safe space for Believers to seek guidance and strengthen their trust in the Lord without ridicule or condemnation for the mistakes they've made."

"That *safe space* should be the church," I mumble.

Verna chuckles. "I know. But until we learn to stop putting each other down, Crown Clinic is there to help."

When I don't respond, she sighs. "Don't worry, Bri, I heard the complaints when I was going to therapy. Deacon James saw the pamphlet in my Bible one Sunday and started railing." She lowers her voice to sound like an old man. "Don't you know that God is the ultimate counselor??"

I snort at her reenactment.

"Yes," Verna admits, "God *is* the ultimate counselor, just as He is the ultimate doctor, and the ultimate provider. But we still go to the hospital, and we still get jobs. There's nothing wrong with Christian therapy, so long as it constantly points you back to Christ Jesus."

I force a smile. "I'll think about going. Or at least I'll start praying more so I don't have to go."

"See?" She smiles brightly. "Crown Clinic is pointing you back to the Lord without you ever even scheduling a session!"

I cackle, then I pull my cousin into a warm hug. "Thank you for always caring, Verna. It's because of you that I'm still a Christian. Or at least trying to be."

She pulls away. "Just trust God, Bri. He's got you."

Verna throws out the burned gravy and we decide to order a

pizza for dinner. I stuff myself with two slices of meat lovers and try to ignore the guilt as I guzzle a cola. I'll work off the extra calories with all the running around I'll be doing for the next three weeks trying to get ready for the convention.

Speaking of which...

I share my Fire & Ice theme with Verna as we split a second cola, still sitting side by side on my couch. She loves the idea and even offers up the phone number of a guy she knew in college.

"He's an old friend I met at campus Bible study, he used to help build the set pieces for the university plays and musicals. I don't know if he's still into all that, but he'll definitely be able to put you in touch with someone who is."

I thank her profusely and tuck the slip of paper with his name and number on it into my back pocket.

Once our second can of Coke is empty, Verna yawns and says her goodbye. I ask Hans to walk her down to the lobby just to give me a moment of privacy. Mercifully, he takes the hint and doesn't return afterward, just stands outside the front door like Bobby used to.

Bobby...

"Where are you?" I whisper, kicking off my jeans so I can put on my pajamas. When my jeans hit the floor, the slip of paper Verna gave me flies out the back pocket. I grab it and move to stash it away inside my bedside table, but as soon as I open the top drawer, I spot my journal and my throat closes up.

Bobby's stupid sticky note is still stuck to the last page of that journal. I don't dare look at it, but I can't stop the sudden pang of emotion that burns through my chest at the memory of it. My phone has no missed calls or texts from Bobby, nothing explaining where he's gone or when he's coming back. It's like he's vanished all over again. The only difference this time is I didn't sleep with him first. But I did feel like we were starting to find common ground.

Okay, we'd argued almost every time we spoke for more than three minutes, but still… the fighting was leading up to something. Eventually, we would have worked things out. Eventually, Bobby would have opened up and told me the truth, and I would have opened up and spoken my truth. That I've missed him all these years. That his disappearance was so hard to get over because I had loved him more than I'd ever loved anyone in my entire life.

That I still love him.

Something wet plops onto my hand and I groan as I wipe at my tears. At this rate, I've cried so much, I'm sure I'm dehydrated.

"Get it together, girl," I tell myself, but I'm not the strong woman I pretend to be.

I grab my phone and sit on the edge of my bed. If Bobby and I will ever work things out, we've got to start getting along. I don't expect him to lower his walls first—it's got to be me.

I owe him an apology for all the drama and fighting I've put him through since his return. I owe him an apology for making him feel as crappy as my mother has made me feel. More than anything, I owe him my forgiveness.

With trembling hands, I dial his number and press the phone to my ear. I don't expect him to answer with a song ringing in his voice, but I *do* expect him to answer. It never dawns on me that Bobby might actually be angry. That he wouldn't want to speak to me. But as the phone rings and rings, I start to realize that maybe he's had enough.

His last words to me roll through my head. *I'm tired of fighting...*

Tired enough to give up?

I take a shaky breath as I listen to the phone. It rings and rings and rings.

Bobby never picks up.

12

I stare at the screen of my phone as Brianna's name flashes across it. *She's calling me.* My jaw instinctively tightens instead of falling slack, like I'm angry instead of shocked. Anger is the last thing I feel right now—frustration, maybe, but not anger in the least.

I didn't leave Bri because of our argument. It was petty and annoying, but I know how she gets when she's irritated so the attitude didn't bother me. After two years together, I've learned all the Gems have a bit of an attitude. Shockingly, Brianna is the one whose attitude bothers me the least. This time, Greyson was the one who got to me.

A man of his word, Grey called me up and *kindly* requested I join him on his trip out of town. I didn't want to go, but I felt I had no choice. Now, I'm standing in one of his warehouses with guards milling about and men who look like construction workers carrying equipment and tools from one end of the room to the other.

My phone still buzzes in my hand as I blink around the

large space. There isn't anywhere quiet I can go to answer this. *Maybe I could step outside*, but before the thought transitions into action, the call ends and the light on my phone goes dark.

Oh well, I sigh. I could send a text to see if Brianna really wanted anything, but it's nighttime right now, she probably called by accident. Instead of bothering her, I send a message to Hans, my backup security, and ask if everything's all good. He replies almost instantly.

Princess had company and then went to bed. All good.

I want to ask who she had in her apartment, but it's better if I don't know. I'm not here for all the romance anyway. I just want to clear my name, earn my forgiveness, and move on. Sure... I'll admit it would be nice to get back with my girl again, but all that's just fancy dreaming right now.

Look at me. Brianna's a millionaire jeweler about to embark on the opportunity of a lifetime. I'm her thug ex-boyfriend turned security guard. I make a fraction of what she brings in—which might seem like a lot for a single guy fresh out of prison, but when you're trying to court the daughter of a billionaire, it's chump change.

On top of that, I'm not on the same level as Bri when it comes to our beliefs. She was a good Christian girl when I met her, and even though I charmed her into making a lot of mistakes in high school, it seems like she's gotten herself together in the last six years. I've noticed the crucifix she wears around her neck; I've seen her praying over her meals, even heard her saying scriptures out loud in the mornings before she leaves for work.

126

Despite everything she's faced, all the bad decisions she's made, she's trying to get it together. I don't want to be the reason she loses any progress. I don't want to be the one to drag her away from God again, even if I'm not entirely sure I believe in Him.

I sigh, cramming my phone back into my pocket. I wasn't good enough for Brianna six years ago and I'm not good enough now. I won't fool myself into thinking I have a chance.

I glance around the warehouse to keep my thoughts from spiraling into dark places. This warehouse holds three vaults the size of sheds, each one is filled with precious rocks and heavily guarded by a team of beefcake men. We're here today to pick out the diamonds Greyson wants to use in his display at The Diamond Industry Convention. His setup sounds cheesy—a table of desserts with the stones set around like treats. I get that the diamonds are chocolate, but the edible theme seems cliché if you ask me.

"I *didn't* ask you," Greyson had reminded me when I'd shared my opinion during the ride over. Six hours in the car together and he'd talked about his precious chocolate diamonds the entire time. Excuse me for thinking I could insert my thoughts on the matter.

All that got me was a quick reminder of my trailer trash roots and a warning to keep my stupid thoughts in my stupid head.

With a sigh, I'd leaned my stupid head against the window and finished the ride in a sullen silence.

I've been standing in this warehouse for most of the

afternoon and evening, watching Greyson's men work. No one pays me any attention, in fact, they walk around me like I'm not even here. It doesn't bother me, but it is annoying to be pulled away from a contract job just so I can mope around a warehouse.

Just then, Greyson saunters over and slaps my back. "Bobby boy," he says with a smile. "We've finally settled on the ones we want. Come have a look."

Without a choice, I follow him across the room to one of the giant vaults. It's entirely made of iron with bars over the door and a crank large enough for two men to handle together. Inside, the room seems to fall to a hush as we cross the threshold. The entire vault is carpeted, and the walls are lined with a velvety material.

When Greyson speaks, his words are devoured by the insulation, I have to lean closer just to hear as he motions to the diamonds resting on the small table in the center of the room. There are other rocks lining the shelves and some in smaller safes on the floor and on the counters around us. From this vault alone, it's evident just how successful Grey's business has become.

"Brown diamonds really aren't all that impressive when it comes to the colored rocks. In fact, they're some of the most common of the bunch." Greyson slips on white gloves and picks up a diamond the size of my thumbnail. "But colored diamonds only make up zero-point-one percent of all diamonds. So even though chocolate rocks are more common than others, they're still quite rare."

I nod like I care, watching in silence as he examines the precious stone. There are rings, studded earrings, and a few loose rocks on the center display—a total of twenty-two diamonds.

"Can you believe these aren't even my best diamonds?" Greyson mutters. It sounds like he's speaking more to himself than to me, but I answer anyway.

"It's smart to put your cheaper diamonds up for bid. You'll profit more since they'll all sell at a higher rate than normal."

He smiles. "You've always been smart, Bobby boy. That's why I'm glad you're my sister's guard."

"I should be guarding her now."

He sets his diamond down and looks up at me. "Do you know why I asked you here?"

"I feel like you're about to tell me now."

"What's my sister been up to?"

"Getting ready for the convention."

He hums and reaches for a pair of studded earrings. "She mention anything about the business? How well its performing."

Honestly, she hasn't. In fact, Bri and I don't speak often, it helps prevent arguments.

"Brianna doesn't share personal details with me," I say professionally.

One of Greyson's dark eyebrows arches. "Really?"

I nod.

"So, all that time alone together and you two haven't..." he lets his voice trail off, leaving the rest of his sentence hanging between us.

I resist the sudden urge to sigh. "I told you I'm not here for that."

He chuckles. "I'm just saying. My sister is a beautiful woman." His deep voice is a low murmur. "As chocolate as these stones. Am I right?"

He's trying to get to me.

I cross my arms over my chest. "What do you want, Grey? I have nothing to report on your sister, and I'm not any help to your diamonds or your display. Just take me back home."

He sets down his earrings. "You are a help to my diamonds."

"How?"

"I told you I wanted you to keep my sister in line with my rules."

"What are your rules?"

He sighs like his next words pain him. "Brianna's been through a lot. You know that. She was stabbed back in high school, and then abandoned by you. That left her depressed for an entire year." He clicks his tongue. "She was so bad; she couldn't attend college. Had to take a year off to get herself together."

My hands slowly curl into fists. This isn't easy for me to listen to, especially since Grey is making it seem like it's all my fault. Saying I *abandoned* Bri when he knows for a fact I was arrested. He's the one who called me before it happened. Said he wanted to do the right thing and give me a heads-up so things would go down smoothly.

I got the call thirty minutes after I climbed out of Brianna's window. I'd just taken his sister on her bedroom floor and then I was being told I'd be going to jail for a crime we both knew I didn't commit.

Without hesitation, I'd turned around and gone back to Brianna's place. I climbed into her window to tell her what was going on, but when my feet hit the carpet, I let out a defeated sigh as I realized there was nothing I could do. Brianna was asleep in bed, still naked with her hair all wild and sprawled over the pillows we'd piled up ourselves.

I didn't want to wake her. Bri had been dragged into mafia drama once because of me, I wouldn't let her suffer through the shame of my arrest. So instead of shaking her back to consciousness, I kissed her forehead and found a sticky note on her bedside table.

What could I say to the girl I loved, knowing I'd be leaving her for a long time?

There weren't any words to explain the sorrow and anger I felt tangled together as one. None of this was fair, but I saw it coming a mile off. With a father like the Colonel and a bloodsucking brother like Greyson, it was only a matter of time before they found a way to get rid of me.

All I could do was scribble down my goodbye and hope that Brianna loved me enough to remember the night we'd spent together. To think of how much I cared for her in her darkest moments, and to know that even though I'd gone, that I would certainly come back for her one day.

I did come back. But it was too little too late. Brianna had been poisoned by her family and then attacked right before I showed up in her life again. The timing couldn't have been worse.

Greyson knows this, which is why he's bringing all this up now and shoving it in my face. "My sister graduated with honors. Can you believe it?"

I don't respond.

"I never thought she'd get over you, but she found the strength to move on. Still, I didn't think she was strong enough to open her own store so soon after graduating, but our parents believed in her and helped front the money for Gem Jewelers." He sighs. "I voiced my objections, but no one wanted to listen. Even offered to take over the business when it became clear that she was struggling. Again, Bri didn't listen."

Greyson reaches for a diamond ring, holds it up and squints as he inspects it. "Everything got worse when she was attacked two months ago."

I exhale slowly, trying to see where he's going with this.

"I offered to take over the business again, considering how bad she is at handling stress and trauma. But, again, she refused."

"She wants to handle things on her own, Grey."

He nods, still focused on the ring sparkling in his grasp. "I know. But that's the thing, sometimes what we want isn't what's best for us." He smiles. "Look at all these diamonds, Bobby. Grey Gems is successful, far more than Gem Jewelers will ever be. But I can make Gem Jewelers successful. I can turn Brianna's business into something extraordinary. She's got a tough location, but I'm up for the challenge."

"It's her store," I say slowly. "She can do all that herself. Without you."

"But I want to do it." He sets down his ring and pierces me with his serious gaze. "I want her store. It's obvious she can't handle it, and I'm tired of reminding her of that."

"So you want me to convince her to hand it over," I say quietly.

He grins. "She loved you once, Bobby boy, I'm sure she'll give in to whatever you say once she looks into those baby blues again."

"She can't stand me," I tell him plainly.

He looks at me like he's disappointed. "You can change that."

"I wouldn't be so confident."

"You seduced her once. Try again."

"Greyson—"

"I always knew you were trouble, Bobby." He lets go of a laugh that's filled with so much arrogance, it takes control I didn't know I had not to punch him in the face. "Everyone said you would ruin the Gem name. That you would bring the mafia to our doorstep, and look… You did exactly that."

"I had nothing to do with the attack in high school and you know it." My voice is a snarl as I step closer. "You and your father locked me up for a crime I didn't commit."

"I don't know." He rubs his chin. "It sounds mighty convenient that you show up again after Bri is stabbed. And then you happen to rescue her from another creep which seals the deal for your contract." Greyson tilts his head to the side. "If I report any of this to the police, they'll think you've been arranging all these attacks yourself."

I shake my head, but not because of the nonsense Grey is spewing. I'm struck into silence because everything he's saying makes perfect sense ... just not in the way he thinks.

Brianna and I got cornered six years ago by a smalltime thug from the Spanish mafia. I was blamed for it. Served time for it. But I had nothing to do with it. I also had nothing to do with the attack two months ago, nor was I involved in the near assault from the grabby guy at the streetlight. But I'm starting to think that Greyson had something to do with it.

He might have been innocent six years ago, but he's just laid the pieces of this puzzle right before me. Every time he's asked Brianna for her business, she's been attacked immediately after. Two months ago, and now the grabby guy I saved her from. What's most convincing isn't even the timing of the attack—it's the fact that Greyson knows about the attack at all.

Brianna never told anyone about what happened with the streetlight guy—conveniently right after having dinner with Greyson. I managed to keep her from going to the police and her embarrassment at almost being the victim of assault once again kept her from going to her family. So how on Earth does Greyson know about it?

Because he coordinated it.

I take a slow step toward him which catches his attention immediately. Good. I want to look him in the eye as I say this.

"You're pathetic," I whisper darkly. "It's been you all along. Hasn't it?"

For a single moment, he looks stunned. Then his surprise melts into cool indifference and he actually shrugs. "You've always been smart, Bobby boy."

"How could you? She's your own sister—"

"She's been ruining our family name since she was a teenager."

"So you tried to have her killed?" I'm nearly yelling now, thankful for all the insulation inside the vault.

Greyson narrows his gaze. "I didn't try to kill her. The goal was to scare her—shake her up so she'd be too flustered to handle the business. I thought she would crack under all the stress and anxiety, but she's refused to give up." He licks his lips. "When I heard you were in town, trying to get her to hire you, I figured I'd take my chances with a second attack. But you intervened."

Now, his calm demeanor cracks, revealing a wolfish grin that almost looks demonic. His mouth spreads widely, revealing perfectly aligned white teeth and pink gums. There is technically nothing wrong with his smile, but with the dark edge in his voice and the way the light glints off his glasses, I can't help but think of the Cheshire Cat as I stare at him.

"You might want to be careful with all your big revelations, Bobby boy. No one but you knows about my involvement. But everyone knows about yours."

I frown. "You know I'm innocent."

"Like you were six years ago?"

My jaw clenches.

"We sent you to prison back then, we can send you there now."

"All of this just to get your hands on her store?" I grate out my words like they hurt to say, trying to stay calm. "And you expect me to just sit quiet and say nothing?"

"I expect you to keep my sister safe."

His words throw me off. I'm so stunned, all I can do is stand there and blink dumbly.

He explains, "I want Brianna's store, but it doesn't have to come to violence and prison time. Use your influence to convince her to sign it over to me. Once the store is in my name, I promise the attacks will stop and you won't be in danger of going to jail." He slaps my shoulder. "I'll even ask my uncle to wipe your record clean."

My heart nearly stops. This isn't a get out of jail free card, it's a fresh start. With a clean record, I won't have a conviction hanging over my head. I won't have to work for companies that specialize in hiring thugs. I won't have to feel ashamed of any part of my past.

But at what cost?

I'd have to convince Brianna to give up her business—to Greyson no less.

The very thought leaves me lightheaded and bilious. First of all, Brianna would never listen to me, not over a decision that serious. Second of all, even if I thought I could influence her, I'd never live with myself for betraying her like that. Earning her trust to get my record cleaned. I'm desperate, but not selfish.

Before I can open my mouth to reject Grey's offer, he holds out his hand to shake mine. I don't take it, but that doesn't stop him from declaring that we have an arrangement.

"I'm glad to do business with you," he says in a chipper voice.

"Greyson, I'm not—"

"Having you by my sister's side is a good thing. Even if you don't manage to convince her, you'll still be there to keep her safe. After all the danger she's faced?" He blows air through his lips. "I'd hate for her to get attacked again. And who knows, if she *is* targeted, maybe your presence won't make as much of a difference as you might think."

Did he just threaten to kill us both?

No. I almost shake my head. *He only threatened to kill* me.

I believe he would do it. With the help of his father, he's already put me behind bars once. What's one more dead thug in the streets? Besides, anyone who's willing to hire someone to stab his own little sister is definitely nuts enough to kill someone he doesn't like and isn't related to.

I guess these are my only options: convince Brianna to give up her business or die trying.

13

The gala is finally here. Goosebumps are scattered over my arms as I stand in front of my full-body mirror. My dress is beautiful, an off-shoulder piece of bright orange at the bust that heats into a fiery red as it tapers down my waist, over my hips. There are multiple splits up the skirt of the dress, making it look like flames swooshing around me as I turn circles in the mirror. It's the perfect garment for my Fire & Ice theme, especially matched with my crystal accented heels and the sparkling diamond necklace draped around my neck— representing the *ice*. My afro hair has been tamed enough to work into an elegantly braided bun, a few loose curls brush against my shoulders each time I turn my head.

I am beautiful. The most gorgeous I've ever been. But it means nothing if my display tonight cannot stand boldly beside my father's and brother's. No one is coming out to The Diamond Industry Convention to see me look pretty, they're coming to bid on beautiful stones and—shamelessly—to gossip about the Gem dynasty.

I haven't forgotten the fact that the Jägers will be here tonight, our greatest rivals. Well … my *father's* greatest rivals. I've only just joined the competition but I'm grateful to be given the opportunity to compete anyway.

This is my chance to show the diamond world what I'm made of. To prove to Colonel Gem that I'm not his failure child. To prove to Greyson that he isn't invincible. And to prove to myself that I am worth something.

It's been a hard year for me. I could list all my struggles and failures from the store to the random assaults, but the truth is that I'm done focusing on the negative parts of my life. I'm done giving so much credit and attention to the things that have only brought me pain and misery.

"I'm starting over," I whisper to myself.

Teetering on my six-inch stilettos, I walk over to my bedside table and grab the Bible inside. I'm not looking for a scripture on healing, I'm reading verses that are uplifting. Ones that remind me of who I am. A child of the Most High God.

"Be with me today," I mutter, running my fingers over the thin pages. I've stopped at Psalms 46:10—the words chill me to my bones.

Be still and know that I am God.

I'm dangerously close to crying—the Word does that sometimes—so I put the Bible on my bedside table and teeter back to the mirror. Once I'm sure I look beautiful, I take a deep breath, grab my clutch, and leave my room.

The rest of my apartment is quiet and empty. I've arranged for a driver to take me to the convention center, Hans is going to meet me there. I haven't seen much of Bobby lately... Since he disappeared that first time, he's come and gone like a distant relative. I see him on weekends, sometimes he stops in after work just to check and see if Hans is treating me well. There have even been times where he's sent me text messages, but it's never been more than a few words. Always curt. Always distant.

I have no idea what's happened with him or why he's so detached all of a sudden, but I don't have time to deal with the confusing emotions that come with figuring out Bobby. I've only just begun to figure myself out, adding my gangster ex-boyfriend to the mix is not a good idea. Not tonight, at least.

My heels clack against the floor as I walk to my front door. I can feel myself beginning to sweat already, even though I haven't even left the apartment yet. *Thank God for deodorant*, I smile, opening the door.

My smile freezes on my face as I step into a massive bundle of roses. The bouquet is so large, I can't see around it, but the voice that drifts over them is unmistakable.

"Ready, Princess?" Bobby asks, lowering the flowers.

I snort out an obnoxious laugh. "What's with the bouquet?"

"They're for you."

He passes them to me, and I get a good look at his clothes for the first time.

To my shock, Bobby's wearing a tuxedo, bowtie and all. His tattoos are almost completely covered, except for the ones on his neck and hands, but he looks handsome, nonetheless.

His shoes are shined, and his corsage matches the color of my dress, a beautiful red flower with starbursts of orange on the outer petals. Even though he looks stunning, I can still see hints of the Bobby I know hiding beneath his pressed suit and tie.

He didn't bother shaving, so he's got a nice shadow on his chin that makes him look far more aggressive than normal. His blonde locks are still sloppy, but he had the decency to pull them back into a little bun that's so cute I could kiss him for it. He's so charming right now, I don't notice that I feel completely calm in his presence, or that I'm actually happy to see him.

Maybe the distance has helped us. Maybe we can make it through the night without going at each other's throats.

"Let me put these in water," I say, turning back toward the door.

Bobby follows me inside and watches in silence as I tiptoe through my kitchen. When I'm done with the flowers, he finally speaks—his voice low and raspy.

"Come here."

I go to him, standing like a child before this massive, handsome creature. The gaze he gives me could melt the ice on my display, yet it's a burning inside that feeds me the courage to look him in the eye.

"Yes?"

"You look beautiful."

I nod, unable to speak.

He leans down and kisses my cheek, his next words

murmured against the skin. "My princess."

"Where have you been?" I ask.

I feel him stiffen before he pulls away and looks down at me. All the pleasant charm and heat from a moment ago is gone now. He's all business. All serious.

"I've been handling odd jobs for my boss."

"At Stronghold Inc.?"

He nods stiffly. "Something like that. Let's get out of here."

On the way, he dodges my questions about his whereabouts and instead distracts me with stories about Hans and some of his more dangerous jobs. When I ask him if Hans is out killing someone tonight, he laughs so hard I have to wait for him to catch his breath before he answers, "No, he used tonight to spend some time with his wife. Sheesh. Ex-gangsters aren't all killers, you know."

I frown. "Sorry."

When we arrive at the convention center, there are cameras, journalists, and reporters waiting at the entrance. I feel myself getting nervous as the driver parks and walks around to get the door; my throat begins to tighten and the noise around me hushes to nothing but a murmur. There are crowds of screaming people standing just outside, but all I hear is my heavy breathing and my erratic heart.

I squeeze my eyes shut, fighting off the anxiety attack I feel uncurling inside me. Fear awakens, it's fangs dripping with the poison of despair—that dark feeling that there is nothing I can do. No help to be found. When it bites into my heart, I am struck with a sudden urge to reach into my purse for my meds, but I ignore it.

I made a promise to start over. I made a promise to stay away from the pills. Right now, I realize I may not be strong enough to keep that promise. Maybe this is a process for me, maybe it's something I have to take slowly instead of quitting cold turkey. Either way, I can't let my nerves get to me right now. Not here.

I feel something tug at my elbow and I open my eyes to find Bobby staring down at me, holding my arm. I have no idea how long he's been speaking or nudging me—I don't even know what he's saying right now as he leans toward me and unstraps my seatbelt, but I nod like I understand and slide across the seats to step outside.

The flashing of the cameras almost stuns me, but Bobby's right beside me, casually sliding one of his long arms around my waist. To everyone watching, he looks like my date trying to get cozy for the reporters, but I know he's only here to keep me from falling flat on my face. My knees feel like water and my legs wobble as I walk, it's honestly a miracle that we make it inside without an incident.

Thank You, Jesus, I pray internally. It may not seem like much, but that was the most difficult thing I've done in a long time.

Pinpricks of sweat break through the pores on my forehead. I want to swipe them away, but I fear smearing my makeup. "I'm going to the restroom," I tell Bobby.

He changes direction to escort me, but I wave him off and

tell him to find Lyla at our display instead. Poor girl got here an hour before me to make sure everything would be in place—I hadn't considered the fact that maybe Greyson and the Colonel came early too. I can only hope they're not giving her a hard time.

In the bathroom, I dab at my face with thin sheets of tissue, then I shamelessly gulp water from the chrome faucet. It tastes like minerals and sends a chill zinging through my body at its earthy coolness. The thought of tossing back a pill crosses my mind but I shake my head and repeat Psalms 46:10 again until my voice stops trembling.

I think of sweet Verna and what she would do right now if she could see me. Probably give me a hug and tell me there's nothing wrong with the medication. That God wouldn't hold it against me for taking a dose. I know her logic is right, but I want to fight this with everything I've got. I know if I can make it through tonight—probably one of the most stressful nights of my entire life (other than getting assaulted, ahem)—without taking any meds, then I believe I can truly face anything.

I'm still nervous when I walk out the lavatory, but I'm in a much better place now. A manageable place. I even find the strength to smile at Bobby and Lyla when I spot them by the Fire & Ice setup.

The ropes surrounding the display have been removed so onlookers can walk right up and take a good look. Bobby is there to make sure no one tries to touch anything; Lyla is there to explain the theme. She's giggling right now, explaining to a bidder how we tracked down a contractor to build the thing in

144

just four days.

"Cost us a fortune, but it was worth it!"

The man nods, staring at the miniature waterfall and the glowing red ice. He turns to walk away, but one of the diamonds catches his eye and he actually reaches for one of the little cards sitting on the table by the display. They're for people to write down their bids and share what they're willing to pay before the actual auction begins. It'll give stores an idea of what to expect when the money starts to flow but we've still got two hours before that portion of the event begins.

Once the man is done writing his bid, he drops it in the bucket on the table and leaves. Lyla, Bobby, and I all exchange goofy smiles as we discreetly hi-five each other.

My display is full of second-hand diamonds passed down from my brother and father and six pieces we managed to buy back from celebrity clients. There's even an engagement ring from a singer who got divorced eight months after the wedding. She was so happy to be rid of the thing (and the husband) she donated it for free as long as we agreed to name the ring, 'Mistake.'

Lyla laughs and twirls around excitedly, her dress flows like the mist of the waterfall beside us. She's wearing the ice to my fire in a garment that's white and crystal blue instead of orange and red like mine. She even went the extra mile and got a short white wig installed—an expensive lace front bob I know she'll only wear this once. It's still beautiful, nonetheless.

"Let's get a hundred more bids!" Lyla sings and then she laughs as Bobby takes her hand and twirls her around once more.

"It's only one bid," says a bored voice beside us.

I look up to find my brother wearing a brown tux and brown framed glasses, a deadpan expression on his face. His hands are in his pockets, making him look casual despite his attire.

"Greyson." I greet him with a nod. "Have you gotten bids yet?"

He smiles, a slow pull of the corner of his wide mouth. "Of course. My team stopped counting after the third dozen."

I know I shouldn't be fazed or surprised, but I can't help myself. Embarrassment floods through me so powerfully, I feel the blush on my cheeks before my brother points it out.

He steps forward and runs his thumb over my cheek. "Don't be so upset, Princess."

The nickname makes me bristle. "You should get to your station," I say, stepping back from his touch.

"I just came to be courteous and say hello. Have you stopped by Father's display?"

I shake my head, feeling embarrassed again—not because I haven't greeted my father, I'm ashamed because of the line I'd have to wait in just to get close to his table. The 'Autumn' themed display is the size of a small maze, filled with actual trees and shrubbery for bidders to walk through and discover the diamonds for themselves. Lyla walked through before the opening and sent me messages about diamond studded leaves falling from the trees, rings decorating the very tips of a branch, hanging like dazzling berries from bushes, and sparkling in the crevices of the thick bark of the trees.

"There's security everywhere, but it is beautiful."

Of course there's security, with diamonds hidden in bushes, it'd be too easy to steal something.

"I haven't had the time," I mumble to Greyson.

He shrugs one shoulder. "Maybe you can stop by my table until the line thins out."

"Uh—" I glance over at Grey's station. There's a crowd, but it's nothing like the mass of bodies around our father's station. Still, it makes me feel so small with just three people blinking at my little display while Lyla tries to flirt her way into their wallets.

"Well?" Greyson asks. "I came to see your setup."

"You came to gloat." My brows flatten. "Don't pretend you actually care about Gem Jewelers."

The laugh he barks out makes goosebumps sprout on my flesh. He finds my statement so funny, he actually tilts his head back and holds his belly. When he's finished, he stares right at me, but I can only see one of his eyes with the light reflecting off his glasses.

"I'm more interested in Gem Jewelers than you think."

Bobby shifts beside me. It's a small movement, shuffling half an inch closer to me, but his nearness is so possessive that I step back and blink at him, unsure if I should be afraid of some secret hidden assassin he just saw in the crowd. The look on his face makes my rising anxiety ratchet up even higher. His jaw is clenched tightly as he glares at my brother, blue eyes sharpened into angry slits in his beautiful face. He's suddenly

147

so mad—so tense—I can see a vein throbbing in his temple. But he doesn't speak. Just glares at Greyson who gazes back so casually I'm almost concerned for his vision.

There's no way he doesn't see how angry Bobby is right now. Unless he's just gone blind.

Greyson picks lint off his tuxedo jacket. "Seems like I've overstayed my welcome."

"You should be getting back to your station anyway," Bobby's voice is barely more than a strangled growl.

"What's gotten into you?" I ask once my brother has finally walked away.

Bobby keeps staring after Greyson. "Nothing."

"Bobby—"

"I said *nothing*," he snaps.

I place a hand on my hip. "First you start disappearing, and now that you're finally here, you're all tense and angry all of a sudden."

He glances down at me, an unexpected flicker of joy on his face. "*Finally* here? Did you miss me, Princess?"

I blush. "You know what I mean."

Bobby sighs. "I can't talk here. Maybe later I'll explain things."

"Really?"

He nods. "Maybe."

It's not a promise or a guarantee but it's more than I've gotten in the past. I'll take it.

With a smile, I loop my arm through his and say, "Even though I don't want to, Greyson is right. We should make the rounds and greet the other store owners. It's considered polite."

Bobby groans. "Shouldn't Lyla go with you?"

"Who's going to sell diamonds while we're away?" I raise my eyebrows. "Have you become a salesman in the last six years?"

He snorts and the smile he flashes melts every chamber in my heart. "I've done a lot these last six years. But selling diamonds isn't on the resume."

To my surprise, Bobby tugs on my arm and guides me through the maze of displays. We wave at Greyson as he charms a lovely-looking couple holding one of the free cupcakes he's giving away as part of his theme. Then we ooh and ahh at a display from a jeweler I've never heard of, it's a 'Spring' themed table with diamonds set in the centers of the potted flowers placed about. We see an 'Ice Cream Shop' display and get a free cup of vanilla ice cream. I'm sure it'll give me gas later.

Just when we decide to head back to our station, someone in the crowd squeals and both Bobby and I turn to find out what's going on.

All at once, the crowd shifts and begins to flow in one direction. I crane my neck to see what the fuss is over, but it's Bobby who spots the source of the commotion, using all six feet four inches of himself to see over everyone's head.

"Wow," is all he says until I elbow him.

"Wow what?"

He looks down at me. "The Jägers are here."

149

They should have been here by now. *The convention started nearly an hour ago, if they really want to attract bidders then it's wise to show up on time…* Those were my initial thoughts as Bobby and I pushed through the crowd, but as we got closer and I saw the famed family for myself, I realized he wasn't talking about the store owner. He meant the franchise director.

A few feet from the Jäger Diamonds display is the former mafia boss himself, Amory Jäger. He took over the business after his father, Uwe Jäger, passed him the reins. I remember reading about it in the newspaper like it was everyday gossip.

New York was a different place ten years ago, when the mafia was still in control. Back then, figures like Amory and the rest of his family were celebrities. I remember seeing articles about him as a kid, I'd binge read the columns of *Teen45Oh!*, the teenybopper magazine that would print PG-13 gossip pieces detailing all the drama about the mafia's 'hottest bad boys.' Of course, my mother never knew I had the magazine stashed away in my room, but I can recall far too many nights staying up late with Verna where we'd pull out the latest issue and fawn over the heartthrob mafiosi.

According to the news, Amory left the country ten years ago when the mafia fell, and law enforcement recaptured the city. I remember the public outrage that rang through New York when it was announced that he hadn't been charged with any crimes despite his gang affiliation.

A decade later and all the hatred and anger has finally died down, probably because its common knowledge that his gangster days are over. Amory's a Christian now. For the last ten years, him and his wife have worked hard to distance themselves from the reputation they'd had here in America.

The rumors say his wife led him to Christ. I have no idea how that happened, especially when she was his captive bride—kidnapped and forced to marry him. But I've heard the stories, how they fell madly in love despite their differences and circumstances, and how that love served as the bridge to God for Amory.

He's a different man now, but all everyone remembers are his days as the boss of the German mafia. How he'd murdered people of rival gangs, how he'd made his authority known throughout the city, and had even used that authority to keep his Christian wife in line. Sometimes against her will.

The crowd is excited by his former self. Excited to be in the presence of someone who had once been so callous. So dangerous. I know Amory Jäger isn't who he used to be, but for some reason, I still find myself getting nervous.

Bobby and I watch in silence as he pushes through the gathered crowd toward his store's table. He moves inch by miserable inch, everyone is squealing and shoving to get a look at the real-life mobster. He's taller than I expect, almost as tall as Bobby, with hair so dark I'm sure its black. It frames his face perfectly, sharp grey eyes that seem to cut through the crowd gathered around him, a square jaw, a smile that threatens to give me heart palpations. He's dangerously handsome for a man in his forties, but it's the woman beside him who catches my eye.

"His wife's here too," Bobby mutters, moving closer.

"Rosa Jäger."

She's a beautiful woman with light brown skin and hair as wild as mine, a reminder of her Black and Italian roots. She had been a mafia princess, and her arranged marriage to Amory had united three different gangs back then. They had called her the *Withered Rose* when she was the queen of New York—but that's a story for another time.

There's a little girl on Rosa's hip, clinging to her like she's afraid, and beside them both is a boy who looks far too much like his father. It's mind blowing to see this family here, despite the fact that they own all 16 Jäger Diamonds stores.

"I thought the owners lived outside the States?" I ask Bobby, but a different voice answers me.

"We do. But it's been a while since my niece and nephew visited New York. We thought it'd be nice to come home for a bit."

I turn to find a handsome man smiling at me. With his red hair and wolfish smirk, I'd never guess he was any kin to Amory, but his sharp eyes are unmistakable. Only the Jägers have that dead serious look, even when they're happy.

"Wolfgang Jäger," the man says, extending a hand. "Franchise Partner." He shrugs sheepishly. "But, more famously, Amory's little brother."

"I know who you are," I say, taking his hand. Who doesn't know who he is?

After ruling New York as one of the most powerful gangs in the city, the Jägers are household names now—as recognizable as movie stars and pop singers.

Wolf turns to greet Bobby, holding out his hand, but Bobby doesn't take it. He just stands there glaring at Wolfgang.

Just as I turn to scold Bobby for his rudeness, he opens his mouth and says, *"Guten Abend."*

Wolf's eyes narrow. *"Wie geht's?"*

"Gut."

Now, Bobby extends his hand and Wolf shakes it, but he pauses, staring at Bobby's wrist as he continues to hold him. I know what he's looking at… One of his many bullseye tattoos. But I'm too shocked by the fact that Bobby just spoke German to make any sense of what's happening right now.

Wolf's grip on his hand tightens and he says something quickly in German. Bobby snaps back an answer, and they dance through a conversation that goes right over my head. I've never heard Bobby speak anything but English. And now he's talking to the younger brother of a mafia boss in his native tongue.

Wolf lets him go. "It was nice meeting you two," he says, his eyes still focused on Bobby.

I force a smile. "Yes. Likewise."

Wolf turns to leave, moving through the crowd that's still gathered around his brother. Neither Bobby nor I speak as we watch him go. We stand in silence, staring at the 'Candy Store' display at the Jäger Diamonds setup. The gathered crowd threatens to rival the mass standing around my father's display. The sight immediately melts away the confusion over Bobby's exchange with Wolfgang. All I'm left with is a burning desire to march back to my table and work my butt off. I'm not going to be left out of this rivalry.

I'll deal with Bobby later.

14

Brianna has been quiet since we bumped into the Jägers. Initially, I thought maybe she wanted to focus on the gala and try her best to sell diamonds while she could. But now that the event is over and we're walking side by side toward her apartment, the awkward silence that's been burning between us all night still sits heavily on our shoulders.

I'm proud of Bri, honestly. She picked up almost 12 million in bids, which means Gem Jewelers walked out of that convention with a check for 6 million bucks—the other six were donated to charity. It may not sound like much compared to her father's store which attracted more than 300 million in bids, leaving them with a check for 150 million once the night was over. But it's a pretty penny when you consider her display featured less than half the number of diamonds as her brother and only cost her 2 million to put together in the three weeks she had. I'd say she had a successful night, made even more victorious by the fact that she was only 4 million shy of Greyson's takeaway.

Grey Gems had triple the size of her display, triple the number of diamonds available, and triple the bids. But after all was said and done, Bri's brother only left the convention with a wallet *slightly* thicker than hers. After grinning and snickering at us all night, he walked out of the gala with watery eyes and cheeks as pink as a little girl's.

"Four million in profit," I mutter, tucking my hands into my pockets.

Brianna glances up at me. "The auction went really well tonight. Better than I thought possible."

I smile at her. "You and Lyla really worked the table. And the display was beautiful."

"We probably earned the least of all the stores invited."

My smile falters. "Brianna, you did your best. Better than you thought you would."

"Still…" she hugs herself as we stop at a light.

"You've got to stop comparing yourself to everyone else."

"I can't help it. I've been competing with Greyson all my life."

My words are almost a growl. "Forget about Grey. He doesn't matter."

Brianna looks at me, but the light changes before she can say anything. I grab her hand as we step off the curb, distracting her even more. We had a good night together, all things considered, I just want to focus on the parts that won't give me a headache.

Unfortunately, Bri has other plans.

Once we finish crossing the street, she tugs her hand away

and spears me with her serious gaze. Her eyes are rimmed with liner and her lashes have been fluffed and extended. She looks gorgeous tonight, all dolled up and pretty. But it's the look on her face now that stops my heart—serious yet vulnerable. Like whatever I say to her could determine the outcome of this night, whether there's a chance at us ever reconciling.

"What's up with you lately?" she asks quietly.

I take a deep breath, ignoring the grumbling New Yorkers who march around us. We've stopped on the sidewalk, staring at each other with a crowd trying to get by. I can hear their complaints as they push past, but neither of us cares. Right now, in this moment, it's just me and Bri.

"There's a lot going on, Brianna."

"You spoke German at the convention," she says.

"I'm German." I shrug. "I grew up hearing the language every day."

"But I've never heard you speak it before."

"I never had a reason to."

She blinks once. "And Wolfgang Jäger? What did you two talk about?"

I sigh. "Brianna—"

"I need answers, Bobby." Her face is frowning, but her voice is shaking. She's put me on the spot and left me with no choice but to come clean. I should have seen this confrontation coming after being bold enough to speak German with the brother of the last boss of the German mafia right in front of her.

Brianna's been bugging me for answers since I walked back

into her life, and I promised I would give them to her when I thought she was in a strong enough state to handle them. I think she is strong enough to know the truth, but now the dilemma is different. My own life could be in danger if I say too much.

Would she believe me if I told her Greyson was behind all the horror she's experienced these last few months? That he hired people to stab her—to hurt and frighten her—all for the purpose of trying to get his hands on her business.

I peel my eyes from the concrete and look at Brianna's face, memorizing every feature. The way her bulb nose wrinkles as she sniffles, the shade of mocha brown in her eyes, just as chocolatey as her nut-brown skin. Her high cheek bones, her full lips, the way they pucker as she licks them.

"Bri," I say softly. I reach for her again, intending to simply take her hand so I can be there to hold her if she buckles at the news. But something over her shoulder catches my attention and instead of grabbing her hand, I snatch her by the arm and into my chest.

Just as I turn us around—so my back is to the street and Brianna is safely in my arms—a car jumps the curb and *just* misses us both.

Bri's eyes are squeezed shut, loose curls of her hair whipping in the wind as the car speeds off. When the coast is clear, she pulls away from me and stumbles toward the curb, staring after the car.

"What just happened?" she whispers.

It could have been a random car that lost control at the

worst possible time. Could have been a drunk driver leaving the convention. Could have been anything, really. But I know what it was.

"It wasn't an accident," I say calmly, my hands balling into fists.

Brianna steps beside me, confused. "What do you mean?"

Greyson threatened to have Brianna attacked and have me killed just to get what he wanted. But that car jumping the curb was different. That wasn't a guy with a knife getting paid to stab someone in a non-lethal area. It was a 2-ton vehicle charging full speed at both of us. There was no telling how severely either of us would have been injured. There was no telling whether I'd have the chance to get Bri out of the way in time.

That car could have killed us both.

Greyson's a liar. My teeth grind together as I exhale hard, nostrils flaring.

Maybe seeing Brianna's success at the convention has made him desperate. Maybe he's angry after watching her take home almost the same amount of money as him. She's the owner of a new store that's dangerously close to failing, her display was a third of the size of his, and her jewels weren't worth half the price of anything Grey had to offer. Yet she stood almost side by side with Grey Gems.

This isn't just about taking over her store, it's about putting Bri back in her place. Making sure she follows Greyson's rules. And his first rule is that he always wins.

"We need to talk," I say in a stony voice. I don't care about

Greyson's threats anymore. It's clear now that no one is safe, no matter what I do. Might as well do what I think will actually make a difference.

Brianna looks up at me with a million questions in her eyes, but she doesn't ask anything, just gives me a sure nod and starts back down the street.

We finish the walk to her apartment complex in silence, passing the doorman and waving hello to the guy manning the elevator. I can tell Brianna is tense, that there is a small sense of dread beneath the curiosity that's fueling her. But she smothers her fears as she steps to her door and pulls out her keys.

Before unlocking it, she turns around and faces me. "Whatever you have to tell me, will it change things between us?"

I stare down at her, wishing I could lie and give her the answer I know she really wants to hear. But it was a lie that started all of this. The lie whispered by her family that I wasn't good enough.

It sucks that I have to unravel everything for her right now, right here, like this. But the truth is all I have to offer. After watching Bri suffer at the hands of dishonest people for all these years, I won't deny her this any longer.

"Yes," I answer, and then I add, "but it doesn't have to."

"I don't know if I want to——" she shakes her head. "Sometimes it's better not to know, right?"

I step closer to her. "You have to decide for yourself."

"I don't want things to change. I feel like they just started getting better."

My eyebrows go up. "Really?"

"We made it through the night without fighting. That has to mean something."

"I'm always going to be here, Bri. No matter what."

She clutches her little purse. "I want the truth. But ... I want to enjoy this for just a little longer."

"Enjoy what?"

I probably should have given her the chance to answer the question, but let's be real, I already knew what she was going to say. So instead of letting her speak and lose her words to the wind, I lean down and kiss her, capturing the confession for myself.

She's surprised by the gesture, gasping against my lips, but I don't back down. I haven't kissed Brianna in six years—and I'm not sure I'll ever get to kiss her again. I want this moment to last forever, a little piece of eternity.

To my own satisfaction, so does she.

It's Brianna who reaches up and cups my face with both hands, deepening the kiss. I can't stop the groan that rumbles through my chest. It's more like a feral growl as I press her against the door with a *thud!* that startles us both.

We jerk away, panting, staring at each other like we don't know *whattheheck* to do now.

"Um," Bri wipes at her mouth, smearing a little of her lipstick. My mouth tastes like the raspberry of her gloss, I have to resist the urge to rub my lips together, licking at the flavor.

"Want to come inside?" she asks.

Sheesh, what a loaded question.

15

Bobby and I stare at each other as we catch our breath. There are so many thoughts crashing through my mind right now, but the only words I can form tumble from my lips like a desperate cry.

"Want to come inside?"

Gosh, he must think I'm so easy right now. He'd kissed me, but I had taken it a step further. And now I'm practically begging him to come in and finish what he'd started—a night six years in the making.

Bobby blinks and then gives me a slow nod. He has no words, just his silent understanding of what's happening between us.

My hands shake as I unlock my door, my heels clack against the floor when I walk inside, slapping at the wall in search of the light switch. Bobby's hand covers my own as he gets it for me, but he doesn't let me go.

I turn around to face him and he steps forward, forcing me back. When my back hits the door, it closes behind me and the lock automatically engages. The sound of the mechanical *click* is like an alarm going off. My heart jolts at the thought of being alone with Bobby once again. Just the two of us. A storm raging between us, but neither of us fighting to control it.

I don't know when he leans down again, I'm only suddenly aware of his lips brushing my own, his hands sliding down my waist as he lifts me from the floor. He laughs into my mouth when he turns and stumbles through the dark kitchen. We're like two idiots, dancing to music only we can hear, laughing at jokes that we haven't even told yet.

Remember that time we made love like it was our last night together?

We trip into my bedroom and Bobby kicks the door shut behind him, I'm only slightly embarrassed by the mess of clothes and junk scattered around. Before any shame can settle in, Bobby sets me on the bed, his hands slide my dress over my head. It falls gracelessly to the floor as he tosses it away and yanks at his tie.

What are we doing? I wonder as he trails kisses down my neck. His mouth is like magic, casting a spell over me—trading this lust for love, this desire for passion. I'm only fooling myself right now, but I suppose that's all I need.

I lose myself in the moment, in the passion that mounts with every kiss. But when Bobby frees himself of his shirt and leans over me, everything suddenly stops. I glance up at him, wondering what's happened. Bobby's eyes are wide and unblinking, staring off to the side at something. I turn slightly, tracing his gaze. In an effort to keep himself from crushing me beneath his weight, Bobby has reached out a hand to hold himself up—it's resting on my bedside table, right on top of the Bible I left out.

My blood runs cold.

I'd made it through the night without taking any pills. Had praised myself on getting further away from the meds, only to be chased down by lust instead.

I cover my mouth with my hand as tears fill my eyes. "What have I done?" I whisper.

Bobby rolls off me. "Bri," he starts, and then he just sighs and runs his hand through his hair, yanking out the ponytail. "We haven't done anything. We didn't cross any lines."

"But we were going to!" I almost shriek.

I hadn't made any effort to stop things. To slow down. To speak up. Inviting Bobby in was my idea—not his. I'd been perfectly fine with everything that'd happened, and I would have been fine if he hadn't stopped.

That's what's so scary. That I had no intention of stopping. That I hadn't been strong enough to say something.

Strangely, it was Bobby who'd pulled the brakes. My mafia ex-boyfriend has more respect for my faith than I do. If my mother could see me now, she'd drown me in a tub of holy water. I shiver at the thought.

"I'm so sorry," Bobby whispers.

"Why are you sorry?"

He brushes a thumb over my cheek, wiping away a single tear. "I don't like being the reason you mess up, Bri. I know how much God means to you. I was the one who pulled you away from Him in high school. To come back after all this time and do the exact same thing..." his voice trails off as he glances away. The breath he exhales is shaky, a startling display of just how much he cares.

I reach up and take his hand, kiss his palm. "It's my fault."

"We're both responsible."

He moves to get off the bed, but I don't let him go. "Please don't leave."

"Bri..."

"I'm not asking you for sex. I just," I hug myself, "I don't want to be alone tonight."

Slowly, he nods and climbs back into the bed. Like we've done this a hundred times, I lay on my side and let him wrap his arms around me. We stay like that for a while, enjoying the quiet, ignoring the tension that's so clearly flooding the room. I don't want to acknowledge all the bad right now. There's plenty of that to last a lifetime.

For this moment, I just want to think about how nice it is to get along with Bobby again. To forget his mysterious disappearance. His mafia affiliation. The struggles of my business. The attacks I've suffered. The meds. My mother. And the mistake we almost made not even moments ago.

I'm so sorry, I pray to God.

I try to cover the sniffle, but Bobby's hearing is better than I realize. He shifts in the bed and pulls me against him. His voice is a murmur, a rumble in his chest I can feel as I lay my head against it.

"Talk to me."

"I messed up. Like I always do."

"We stopped. That's all that matters."

"But what if we hadn't?"

He pauses. "I promise I won't ever let it get that far again."

"Again?" I lift my head to look up at him. "So, is this going to be a regular thing?"

Bobby smirks, it's beautiful even in the darkness. "Only if you want it to be."

"I do," I admit. "I want us to start fresh."

He senses my hesitation, running his hand up and down my arm as encouragement. Goosebumps pebble the flesh he skirts over, from my elbow to my shoulder. I pull the blankets against my bare breasts and sigh.

"We need to clear the air before we move forward."

Bobby doesn't speak, still running his hand up and down my arm.

"Bobby," I whisper. "Tell me the truth."

"It'll change everything." His voice is raspy.

"I still want to know."

I feel him nod, his head pressing into the pillow. "At the convention, I spoke German to Wolfgang because I knew he would see the bullseye tattooed onto my wrist when I shook his hand. I guess I was just trying to beat him to the punch. Once he noticed it, he asked me a question."

"Which was?"

"Whether I was ever in the Hunting Grounds."

The German mafia.

I hold my breath as I wait for him to continue, but he doesn't, forcing me to ask, "Were you?"

Bobby sighs. "Six years ago, I wasn't."

"Are you today?"

"No, Brianna, I'm not."

My chest almost implodes from all the pressure. I hadn't realized just how badly I'd wanted his answer to be 'no.'

I sit up in bed beside him, wanting to look him in the eye. Moonlight casts into the room from the window, letting shadows curl over the side of his face. I can just make out the icy blue of his eyes under the ashen light.

"My parents had always suspected—and then when we were attacked together, and you didn't defend me, I just... I panicked. I thought maybe my mom and dad were right. But deep down—"

"I know," he interrupts. "I don't blame you, Bri. We were just kids back then and you were facing so much. Pressure from your parents, rumors about my family, recovering from the attack itself." He pauses to look at me seriously. "I had nothing to do with that attack, Bri. I should have defended you. I should have fought—but I got spooked. I failed you. But I never betrayed you."

"What happened?" I ask him earnestly. "Why did you disappear right after? Why did you leave me?"

"It wasn't because I was done with you," he whispers.

I turn away as tears start to burn the backs of my eyes. Until this very moment, it'd never crossed my mind that Bobby had left for other reasons. I'd always stuck to the story my parents had fed me, that he'd dumped me and moved on. That he'd returned to the mafia. It was easy to believe the lie when I was

168

reeling from the attack and drowning in heartbreak over his absence—no matter the reason for it.

Now that the truth is coming out, I feel like I can't take the pain that comes with it. I'd been wrong about Bobby all along. And he'd still come back anyway, had still tried to reconcile. Had even continued to love me.

Just to keep from crying in front of him, I scoot over and open the drawer on my bedside table. That pathetic sticky note is still stuck to the back of my old journal. I tear it loose and turn back to Bobby. The paper is gripped so tightly in my hands, it quivers as I pass it to him.

"I kept it."

He sucks in a breath. "After all these years?"

"I couldn't let it go."

"Bri…" He closes his eyes. "I wrote this because I thought I'd never see you again."

"What made you think that?"

He takes a breath, balling the paper up in his fist. I whimper as I watch him destroy it, but I don't stop him. Bobby's back now, and he's brought the truth with him. There's no reason to hold on to the pain of the past anymore.

When he lets go of the deep breath he'd taken, Bobby tells me everything. How my father and brother had him framed for the attack we'd both suffered. How he went to prison for four years and then spent another two hiding out from my family, afraid that one day they'd come for him again. Lock him away just because they could. Then he tells me about Greyson and his connections to the attacks I've suffered. How he's had Bobby reporting to him, delivering updates about my behavior and my business.

When he finishes, I'm no longer fighting back burning tears, I'm resisting the urge to climb out of bed and go rip my brother's head off.

How dare he have me chased down and stabbed just to scare me into giving up my business???

He has no idea what he's done to me. The scars I've suffered from that assault, from the grabby man on the corner, and from the car that just jumped the curb. I've been hopped up on meds for anxiety, hated by my mother because I can't keep it together, and mocked throughout the diamond realm for how pathetically my business has been performing.

Do you know how difficult it is to run a million-dollar company while taking meds, fighting a psychological disorder, trying to get along with your overbearing mother, and still attempting to hold on to *some* sort of relationship with God?

It isn't easy. And I've had no slack, respect, or support along the way.

But none of that compares to the trauma Bobby's faced over the years. Four years in prison for a crime he didn't commit, banished from ever seeing the woman he loved, and threatened with more prison time hanging over his head all day, every day. All while living with the knowledge that everyone around you thinks you're a lying gangster who turned on his girlfriend in high school.

"You had no choice but to join the Hunting Grounds when you were in prison." I stare at the bullseye tattooed onto

170

his wrist. There are others all over his body. One for each kill he performed in prison—hits on rival gangs, guys his friends didn't like, even a couple guards who'd made his higher-ups angry. I can't count them all.

"You had to do horrible things, or else they would have killed you."

He nods. "But that doesn't make it right. I still killed people. I stole from people. I lied to people." He sighs. "I'm not a good person. Your parents were right—I've never been good enough for you."

I frown, reaching up to grab his face so I can make him look me in the eye. "I don't care what my parents think. They can't stop me from loving you."

He shifts uncomfortably. "What about what God thinks?"

The question makes me pause.

My voice comes out weakly. "I've only ever loved you, Bobby…"

Would God be unhappy if we stayed together?

Bobby grabs my hands and pulls them from his face. He kisses each one. "Have there been others?" he asks almost shyly.

I shake my head. "There's only been you."

He nods. "All this time."

In six years, I haven't dated any other man. I wasn't waiting for Bobby, but I certainly hadn't made room for anyone else in my life. It just didn't feel right, and whenever my wretched mother did manage to get me to go out with some sad guy she met at church, the dates usually ended horribly, or I would totally chicken out and not bother going.

There's only been Bobby, despite him not being here. As if my heart had known all along that he would eventually return. But his presence in my life doesn't change the fact that there's still a wall between us.

Bobby isn't saved, and the Bible is clear on Believers dating non-Believers. I made a mistake in high school, but I'm older now. Wiser now. I know better now. Which means there is no excuse.

Bobby brushes his thumb over my knuckles, gaining my attention. "Bri, you're worth the change. I just..."

I pull my hands away. "Don't do that, Bobby."

"Do what?"

"Don't even entertain the idea of getting saved just for me."

He looks bewildered. "I thought that would make you happy."

"It would. But only briefly. If you give your life over to God, it must be because you want God for yourself. Not because you want me to sleep with you."

His jaw clenches. "I'm trying to get my life together, Bri. Maybe this is part of the plan. Maybe it's something I've thought about *before* I had you naked in bed."

I suddenly feel exposed. Ashamed.

Bobby glances away as I lift the blankets to cover myself, awkwardly aware that he's only in his boxers and I'm in nothing but my lacy panties.

"Have you thought about this before now?" I challenge

him.

Bobby's brows flatten. "Not really."

I slide out the bed and pad over the floor to my dresser. I'd really like to put on more clothes now.

"We can talk about our beliefs later. You don't have to decide something like this right here, right now," I say, sliding an oversized sleepshirt over my head.

"I just want you to know I'm not against it."

"I believe you."

"Bri…" Bobby takes my hand once I climb back into bed. "I'm glad you believe what I told you."

How could I not? When I line up the evidence, the timeline makes it clear. Every time Greyson and I have talked about my business, I've been attacked right afterward. That's not strong enough evidence to prove anything in court, especially not with him and Dad holding Uncle Lee—the police commissioner— in their back pocket. But it's enough to convince *me*. I know it in my heart because I know my brother, how competitive and callous he can be.

"Greyson can't get away with this," I say firmly. "He's ruined so much of my life for his own selfish gain. It isn't fair."

Bobby presses his lips together.

"You look like you have something to say."

"It won't be easy, but if I can find irrefutable evidence against Greyson, we might be able to make him pay." He meets my gaze, and then blushes. "Legally, of course."

I almost laugh. "I want him to go to jail, not die."

"I'll do whatever I need to do to make that happen. But if

he suspects me, things could get seriously dangerous."

He's had someone assault me multiple times and could have had me killed with that car incident. I believe Bobby when he says we might be in over our heads. But I'm not going to back down from this.

I take a deep breath. "God will protect me."

Bobby just nods silently.

Okay … I'll admit, I've got some praying and repenting to do tonight, but God isn't human. He isn't fickle and petty. He loves me enough to still protect me, to never fail me, even though I've failed Him countless times. And I love Him enough not to make this mistake again. If I'm starting over then it'll be completely—not just with the meds, but with Bobby too. I want to do things the right way. God's way.

"Bri, I'm with you one-hundred percent," Bobby says. "I just want you to know what you're getting into. What this means for your family."

My father was willing to frame Bobby for a crime he didn't commit just to protect our reputation. Imagine what he'll be willing to do to keep our family name from being stained by an arrest. If word gets out about Greyson's dirty work, everything will crumble. My business might even take a hit.

My hands ball fists into the blankets. "The last six years of my life have been a nightmare. Revealing the truth might be rocky, but it can't be worse than anything I've already experienced." I look at Bobby. "I'm doing this."

He smiles. "No, Brianna, *we're* doing this."

That's right. I'm not the only one Greyson's hurt. I'm not

the only one he's willing to get rid of just to get what he wants. We're in this together, we always have been, despite six years of separation and lies. We were never truly apart, just a little lost—like we'd taken a wrong turn on a journey that was already written in stone. Our fates sealed. Our destinies forever entwined.

Bobby and I are meant for each other, we've just got to get the filth out of the way first. Then everything will fall into place. I know it will.

16

Brianna snores softly in her bed. She basically ordered me to put my clothes back on after our conversation and forbade me from sleeping over—not even on the couch. I'm not offended by her standards, since she's trying to take her faith seriously and all that. I suppose I can't blame her. It's my fault she's uptight about the whole thing anyway; I'm the one who initiated the kiss in the hallway, and I initiated everything between us six years ago.

Brianna had been good and righteous and pure, and—yes—I know she had a choice in everything we did, but I never made the choice easy. It'd been my goal to drag her as far away from her cushy Christian life as possible.

To be honest, I didn't have anything against her faith at all. I'd never even thought about God and all that. All the animosity and resentment I felt had been against Brianna's upbringing.

The idea that she was somehow inherently better than everyone else *because* she was Christian made me burn with anger. Her parents had poisoned her, had tainted her faith more than I ever had. Because they took the humility they preached about and made it a prideful badge of honor. Looking down on everyone who wasn't like them, everyone who didn't think, act, or speak as righteously as they did.

I was a filthy sinner in their eyes, and everything wrong in Brianna's life was because of me—not because she was human and had made her own mistakes. Just like everyone else. I guess I just wanted to prove that they weren't as perfect as they thought, and that their imperfections weren't because of me.

The Gems had deep-seated problems well before I came along. The Colonel had always been an unlovable brute, Mrs. Gem had always been insufferable, and Greyson's always been ... Greyson.

If there had been any real hope for those godforsaken people, it had been in Brianna. And I'd snatched that away from them.

It wasn't until she freaked out when we'd almost had sex that I realized just how serious our high school antics had been. I'd corrupted Bri and left for six years, but she had stayed and dealt with the guilt, the condemnation from her parents, the persecution from her church, and the emotional heartbreak. All the dark shadows hidden beneath the shiny lure of our sins.

I stare at her from across the room as she sleeps peacefully. I'm sitting in the comfy chair she's got tucked into a corner, piled high with throw pillows and laundry. The room is dark, but I've been here long enough for my eyes to have adjusted, I can make out Brianna's form beneath her heavy blanket. I can hear her deep breathing. I can pick up every movement she makes—every little shift in the bed, adjusting against the pillows, yanking the covers over her body as she rolls over.

I am completely aware of everything about Brianna, refusing to take my eyes off her. I have memories of sitting in her bedroom back in high school, when she'd let me sneak in through the window at night. We'd make out for a while, but she'd always stop me before things got too heavy, then she'd banish me to the chair in the kiddie corner as she settled for bed. She rarely trusted me enough to let me sleep beside her—probably a good idea.

Those nights had been innocent and sweet. Two kids hiding from their parents, whispering secrets until sunrise. I didn't think much of those nights when they were actually happening; after watching her sleep for hours, the most I ever got out of it was the chance to tease Brianna about farting in her sleep the next day at school. But now, it feels so different. I'm not just sitting here while she sleeps, I'm watching over her. Protecting her. Something I would've done without the pay.

I messed around with women when I got out of prison, but it was never anything serious. Never anything that kept me up afterward like this. I have never cared to watch over anyone else. Never wondered if any other woman was alright, if she was sleeping okay, if she was dreaming. And if, somehow, I was in her dreams. Before tonight, I'm sure if I showed up in any dream of Bri's, I would've been a villain. Now, I'm hoping my presence means something else.

I take a deep breath as I rise from the chair. I've been sitting for long enough, if Bri wakes up to use the restroom, she'll be pissed to find me still here and probably never let me into the apartment again. I walk slowly across the room and kiss her on the cheek. As I pull away, I glance down and see her Bible sitting on the bedside table.

It's the same leatherbound Book she carried to church when we were kids. I remember holding it for her whenever she got lazy, boredly flipping the pages as her pastor droned on through her sermon. I have no idea how many times Bri dragged me out to church with her, but I know I've gone enough to remember a few scriptures.

The Bible, Christianity, Faith—none of that has crossed my mind in six years. In prison, there was no room or time for God. He doesn't care about guys like me. Personally, I don't blame Him. My cellblock was full of murderers, rapists, thieves, and everything in between. There was no God to rescue us because we didn't have souls to save.

I slide my gaze over to Brianna, still sleeping in bed. She wouldn't believe any of that for a second. She'd probably scold me for thinking so darkly about myself, for daring to believe that I had no soul and that it wasn't worth saving. We never really talked about my beliefs while we were together, probably because I'd willingly gone to church with her whenever she'd asked. She just assumed I was on the same page as her, despite my obvious rebellion.

The few times we did talk about my faith, she would get angry at my questions and challenges, but she'd always end the conversation with the same line.

"Jesus still loves you, Bobby, no matter how you feel about Him."

Her words still ring in my heart today, so strongly that I shock myself by reaching for her Bible and peeling open the first few pages. I'm not a church boy by any means. But I can't stop myself from flipping through the Book, like I'm looking for something. I have no idea what I expect to find, but my fingers move without guidance, almost acting on their own.

There is a tug deep inside of me, I feel it gripping my heart, growing tighter with each page I turn. It only releases me when I find what I've been unknowingly searching for.

The scripture I've stopped at is one of Brianna's favorites.

Before I formed you in the womb I knew you, before you were born I set you apart; I appointed you as a prophet to the nations. **Jeremiah 1:5 NIV.**

Obviously, I'm not a prophet. But the meaning of the words still makes my heart skip a beat. Could I be so special to God? Known and set apart. Though I had felt so forgotten and alone while in prison. Abandoned and betrayed by Brianna and everyone else. In contrast, I didn't feel God's presence either but, admittedly, I'd never searched for it.

I could now. I could give it an honest try. Not just for Brianna or even for curiosity's sake. I could do it for myself. To right all the wrongs of my past, to shine some light in the darkness all around me.

But…

I set the Bible down with a sigh. *That's enough for today—*

enough for the *week* if you ask me. This morning, I wasn't even sure if I believed in or cared about God. Now, I'm reading the Bible and feeling all special inside.

Get a grip, I tell myself, heading for the door.

17

I didn't notice my Bible had been left open until I went to read it. I hadn't read it before falling asleep the previous night, which meant only one person could have been browsing the Book of Jeremiah while I slept.

I'm not surprised to find Bobby on my couch when I leave my bedroom, but I am shocked to see him half-naked and soaking wet. He's wearing nothing but a shamefully tiny towel tied around his waist. It hangs helplessly from his hips as he turns towards me, wiping blonde bangs from his eyes.

"Uh," is all I can manage as I stare at him.

He laughs awkwardly. "I left early this morning, but I didn't think I'd have time to shower and change and make it back here before you left for work."

I frown. "Wait … are you saying—"

"I grabbed a change of clothes from home and came back here."

"You used my shower?" I fold my arms across my chest, more stunned than angry.

He nods. "I brought my own shampoo. If that helps."

I can't help but laugh. "Bobby, if you're going to be late just send me a text. You don't have to fight through morning traffic and shower in my bathroom just to be here on time."

For a moment, he looks embarrassed, but he covers the expression with a sweet smile. "Thanks, Bri."

"You can leave your dirty clothes here. I'll toss them in the wash before we leave."

"Sounds good."

"Did you leave me any hot water?"

His cheeks dimple. "Of course."

When I'm done with my shower, I smell coffee and breakfast being cooked in the kitchen. Not for the first time, I thank God for a security guard who knows how to cook and is dedicated enough to actually do it for me. As I sit at the counter and eat the pancakes Bobby serves me, I let myself wonder what life would be like if he stuck around after his contract ends. The thought makes my forehead wrinkle.

There's only one reason Bobby would stick around after his job is over. But after what happened last night, and everything we discussed, I'm not sure if he has a place in my life—whether he sticks around or not.

As if he's reading my mind, Bobby plops onto the barstool beside me and sighs. Neither of us speaks for a moment. I have no idea what to say, and Bobby's busy stuffing himself full of the chocolate chip pancakes still sitting on my plate.

"I don't know why you didn't just make enough for yourself," I joke.

He chuckles and it feels like the tension in the room just cracked. Bobby shatters it with his smile. "You never eat all your food, Princess."

He's right. Even in high school, Bobby would finish his own food and then clean my plate. It didn't matter if we were eating sloppy joes in the cafeteria or dining out with our friends. I'd gotten used to seeing Bobby's cheeks stuffed with my leftovers, the sight of him pouring more syrup over my pancakes now leaves a warm feeling swelling in my chest.

I sigh and lean my head against his broad shoulder. "I left my Bible out on the bedside table last night."

He stiffens but keeps eating.

"I don't remember reading in Jeremiah before bed."

Bobby hums as he reaches for my glass of apple juice.

"Did you read it?"

I have to wait for him to swallow before he answers plainly, "I did."

His response makes me smile, but I keep myself calm. Reading the Bible doesn't make you Christian—even Satan knew the Word enough to quote it back to Jesus Christ Himself. He twisted the words, of course, but the point is that he knew it. It isn't enough for Bobby to read the Bible; he's got to believe and accept it too. But I can admit this is a good start.

"Why'd you read it?" I whisper.

Bobby sighs. "To be honest, I don't know. I saw it sitting there and I reached for it without even thinking." He swivels on the barstool, forcing me to sit up as he faces me and looks me right in the eye. "I'm not making any promises, Bri. But I'm trying—not just for you. I'm trying for myself, just like you said."

A smile slowly takes over my face. "Did you like what you read?"

"It left me with more questions than answers, to tell you the truth."

I laugh. "That's not uncommon. But it shows that you're thinking about what you're reading, not just letting the words pass before your eyes."

"I guess that's worth something."

My morning conversation with Bobby leaves me in a good mood throughout the day. I get to work with a smile on my face, and when I send Lyla off to deposit our check from the convention, the smile grows even wider. I actually stare at the screen of my computer until the balance on the company's account changes right before my eyes. I could cry from all the blessings I've gotten lately. It's almost like a dream, which quickly turns back into the normal nightmarish reality I'm used to when my brother walks into my store.

My jaw literally falls open at the sight of his smirking face coming toward me. Thankfully, there are two customers in the store when he arrives, so I have an excuse to ignore him for a few minutes while I finish up their orders. He spends the time examining the diamonds on display, shaking his head at the jewels like he's disappointed. Once the customers clear the store, he saunters over to me and splays his hands on the glass box before him.

"Brianna."

"Greyson."

"Last night was amazing, wasn't it?"

"Indeed."

His smile falters, upper lip quivering as he tries to maintain the fake expression.

I decide to get straight to the point. "What do you want, Grey?"

"Come have lunch with me."

After everything Bobby told me, I'm a little wary of having lunch with my brother. In fact, the only thing keeping me from reaching for the pepper spray I keep behind the counter is the fact that I know Bobby's out there somewhere watching. I have no idea where exactly he's standing, but he's been my security guard long enough for me to trust that he's well aware of Greyson's presence in my shop. I know there's no way he'd ever stand by and let him hurt me.

I also don't think Grey is bold enough to try something in broad daylight. Every attack I've suffered has been at the hands of hired help. My brother is too good or too afraid to do anything himself.

I realize he's still waiting for an answer when a sigh fills the air. Grey takes off his glasses and polishes them with the handkerchief from his breast pocket. He's wearing a nice suit with a tie I know his sad wife picked out. It's dark green and has awful flowers printed on it, the sort of tie I'd expect a man twice his age to wear.

"Bobby's in the alley across the street," Grey says matter-of-factly. He carefully puts his glasses back on, setting them on the very edge of his round nose. "He'll follow you to the restaurant, like a good little guard, and make sure you don't die along the way."

My gaze narrows. "Should I be worried about dying along the way?"

"Why do you sound so accusatory?"

I shake my head. Now is not the time to confront him about the attacks. Instead of answering, I focus on the computer at the checkout counter and organize a few orders we received online. One for a pair of diamond earrings I'm happy to get rid of, and another order for a huge engagement ring that makes me burn with jealousy.

I've never been much of a romantic, but I've always wanted love in my life. With things seemingly working out with Bobby, I can't help but fantasize about our future together. About us picking out rings from my own store one day.

I shake my head, remembering that my stupid brother is still standing right in front of me, waiting for a reply. "I'm guessing you have lunch reservations?" I say.

Greyson nods. "Come on, you can text Bobby the address."

It disturbs me that he knows exactly where Bobby's located and mentions him casually, like he isn't double crossing him and forcing him to spy on me. Imagine… my own brother is responsible for all the pain I've experienced these last few months, all so he can get his hands on a business he's constantly saying is beneath him. The realization makes me bristle as I ride in Greyson's car to the restaurant he's picked out.

I text the address to Bobby, not bothering to explain anything further. He's a smart man, and I know he saw me leave the store with my brother. It doesn't take long for Bobby to put things together.

You good?

I stare at his message as I slide into the chair across from Greyson. He orders our drinks and appetizers and then starts bragging about how well his display performed last night while I punch out a reply.

It's just lunch. I'll be fine.

I'm outside if you need me.

Go eat. We might be awhile.

He doesn't text me back, but I don't worry about it. Greyson might be evil, but he's the type of evil who cares far too much about his reputation to do anything stupid. That gives me the perfect opportunity to have a serious talk with him.

I spear my brother with my meanest glare as a waiter serves us our drinks and matching Caesar salads.

He raises an eyebrow at my expression. "Something on your mind, sister?"

"You know exactly what's on my mind."

"If I knew, I wouldn't be asking. Would I?"

"Tell me, Greyson, have I ever done anything to offend

you?"

His eyebrows pinch together, making the thick skin of his forehead bunch into rolls. "What are you talking about?"

"I'm asking what I've done to make you want to kill me."

Now he gets it.

Greyson clears his throat and slowly sets down his fork. I watch him in silence as his anxiety seems to heighten right before my eyes. His shoulders tense as he inhales, nostrils flaring wide. I can see the way his throat bobs when he swallows, the way his eyebrows seem to flatten and the rolls in his forehead slowly smooth out. I can see every dotted pore on his forehead, puckered and swollen as nervous sweat pushes through.

I have blindsided him. Good.

"Brianna—"

"You hired people to come after me."

"I don't know where you're getting this from."

"Did you really think you could use Bobby against me?"

All at once, realization storms into the room and the truth hits Greyson hard. His eyes widen as he begins to understand, and I see the moment his arrogant demeanor slams back into place. As if he's suddenly been rid of all his problems.

He leans over the table, a teasing grin on his face. "So, Bobby boy let the cat out of the bag." He tsks. "I had hoped he would be smarter than this."

My heart stops. I'm such an idiot. I went into this conversation with the confidence that Greyson wasn't foolish enough to hurt me in a public place, but there is nothing stopping him from doing anything to Bobby. With the help of my father, he's had him arrested once before. I'm certain he can do it again—or worse.

Greyson senses the shift in the air, picks up on my anxiety like a moth drawn to a flame. Or a vampire who's just smelled fresh blood. When he licks his lips, I swear the sound he makes is sickeningly close to a hiss. He's always been a snake.

"You and Bobby been talking?" he asks casually. "I thought you hated him after he got you stabbed and then left."

"He didn't get me stabbed," I say icily.

Greyson licks his teeth. "And who told you that?"

"Let's cut the crap, Grey."

He jerks forward, grabbing my wrist before I realize he's even moved. "Let's cut the crap, indeed." His grip tightens. "Have you and Bobby been talking?"

"Let go of me."

"No."

I glance around, searching for any waiters or nearby diners to help me, but there's no one. Greyson's picked out a table tucked into the corner of the restaurant. The closest customers would have to stand and crane their necks to peek over the chairs and find us.

"Answer the question," Greyson threatens.

I wince. "You're hurting me, Grey."

"And you've been hurting this *family* since you first met Robert Eckhardt."

"That's not his name anymore." My words are a low growl, daring him to argue with me. "He goes by *Ackard*. He hasn't been an Eckhardt since he was fourteen years old."

Greyson shrugs. "Changed his name but not his nature."

"You don't know anything about his nature."

"You're right." He releases my wrist. "I thought he valued his freedom."

I clench my jaw. It was a mistake to confront Greyson like this, but I didn't come to this lunch without a plan. Bobby and I said we would work together, but I don't trust him not to take the fall if things go south. I don't trust that he would let me carry my own weight. Bobby would take every sin onto himself; he would bear my cross for me. He's already been punished for sins he didn't commit; I won't let him suffer again.

Greyson is my brother. That makes him my problem.

I lift my chin. "Bobby does value his freedom. And I value my life. In exchange for both, I'll give you my store."

My brother stares at me, greed and apprehension flickering in his eyes. He wants to take the offer but isn't sure if I'm bluffing or not.

"Bobby and I are in love. All we want is to be together without any drama. He wants to get away from his mafia past and I want to get away from my failing business. Just leave us alone, Greyson. The business in exchange for peace."

He licks his lips. "I want it signed over tomorrow morning."

That's not enough time.

"Give me a week—"

"Three days."

"I need to speak with my lawyer, Grey."

He nods slowly, and I take advantage of his silence to reach into my purse and slide an envelope over to him. Inside is a check for four million dollars. Every penny I made at the gala. It might not be much to Greyson, who earned his first billion two years ago, but it means the life or death of my business for me.

Greyson knows this, which is why he sucks in a gasp as he lifts the check from the envelop and stares at it, open-mouthed.

"A token of good faith," I say, rising from my chair. "In a week, you'll have everything else, but until then, no more assaults and no more arrests."

He nods, still staring at the check. He isn't engrossed by the amount, that's actually quite a small bit of money for Grey—it's the fact that I'm willing to give it up that's got him enchanted. He has a real chance at snagging my business. At least that's what he thinks.

I turn to walk away, but Greyson calls after me, "You're doing the right thing, Brianna."

I agree. But for a completely different reason.

18

Brianna sighs over her lunch for the third time, making me glad that I decided to join her at her favorite tapas bar. She'd texted me and said we needed to talk—the teenager inside of me had hoped she meant to talk about us, but after seeing the depressed look on her face, I'm hoping it's something else that's bothering her.

When the cheese melted over her taquito begins to solidify, I figure it's time to speak up. We've been sitting in this painful silence for long enough.

"What's going on, Bri?"

She glances up at me. "I'm sorry, Bobby."

"What happened?"

She's been uptight since she had lunch with her brother yesterday. I knew I should have gone inside, but I thought she needed a moment with her family. I thought giving her some privacy would be for the best. But ever since she left the restaurant with Greyson, she's been distant. Not in a way that makes me feel like I'm the problem, it seems like the issue is something else entirely, and that's what worries me.

I can fix things when she's angry at me. Apologize, give her some space, and make it up to her with chocolate chip pancakes later on. But when it's something else, something I have no say or control over, that's when I feel helpless.

I run my hand through my hair, then remember that it's tied back in a bun and my hand stops abruptly. I sigh. "Bri…"

"We have a week to gather intel on Greyson."

I blink at her. "What?"

"We need to move quickly—"

"Why do we have to do it in a week?" We hadn't even talked about our plans since the night of the convention. Honestly, we haven't talked at all. Bri's been acting so weird. Now, I'm starting to understand why.

I shake my head before she can answer my first question. "What happened at lunch with Greyson?"

Brianna's mouth flattens into a line. She's wearing a simple ivory dress that seems to make her dark brown skin glow, but right now I can't see past the scowl on her face. It's such an odd expression, a look of pure disdain which molds into sympathy as her gaze lifts to meet mine.

The disdain, I understand. But the sympathy is new. Since when has Brianna ever felt sorry for me? Until a few days ago, she thought I was secretly responsible for the assault and attempted rape she faced six years ago. She's been kinder since learning the truth, she's apologized for hating me and blaming me, but she's never been sympathetic. Whatever semblance of pity she had turned into hatred and anger toward her brother.

That's the fuel we used to conjure the idea that we could corner Greyson. That, somehow, we could make him pay. We could right all the wrongs he's committed.

At the time, it was just hopeful pillow talk. But I can see now that Bri's been thinking about it. Seriously thinking, to the point that she's done something crazy because of whatever little plan she had going on in her own head.

Leave it to Brianna to go off on her own.

She's always been stubborn like this. Headstrong. Independent. All the things that would drive me crazy and leave us in a screaming match back in high school. And all the things that would drag my sorry butt back to her the next day, whispering desperate apologies as I kissed her like she was the only woman in the world.

I almost laugh as I watch her fumble for words, trying to think of a way to tell me she's done something horribly wrong.

"Just spit it out, Bri," I tell her.

She exhales slowly, and then, as if she's changed her mind, she shakes her head and smiles. "I've got something for you."

Because I'm a sucker for gifts, I pretend I don't notice the shift in conversation and raise my brow at her. "What is it?"

She pulls out a small rectangular box and passes it to me. I honestly have no idea what to expect, so I grab the package and lift the lid with held breath. When I see what's inside, I let go of a laugh.

"You bought me a Bible."

It's one of those pocket Bibles, only containing the Book of Psalms, Proverbs, and the New Testament. Shockingly, I used to have a hundred of these lying around my house. Bri's church would hand them out during big events when people who weren't regular members would show up. It was always the youth group's job to pass them around, standing at the doors or out on street corners, trying to get uninterested people to take home a free Bible. I hated going to those events, but Bri would always beg me to go, and I'd promise to behave as long as she made out with me afterward.

When I close my eyes, I can still smell the lavender scent of her shampoo from those days when I'd pin her against the wall and kiss her as she giggled.

"Bobby, we *shouldn't…*" She would always pretend she didn't want me.

"You promised," I'd murmur between kisses. "Remember, Princess?" And then she would laugh again, and I'd kiss her again. "You promised…"

Oh, the joys of young love.

Now, the little Bible brings a smile to my face. Because I know Brianna isn't giving it to me with the promise of a sweet kiss later on, she's giving it to me with the promise of everlasting love. From her and from her Father.

The gift means more to me than she can imagine. The fact that there is someone who doesn't just care about me or my heart or my emotions—Brianna cares about the state of my soul. I have no words to thank her. None that would be enough.

Brianna reaches across the table to hold my hand. "I wanted you to have one."

My fingers interlock with hers. "Thanks, Bri."

Even though I know there's more for us to talk about, something that Brianna isn't telling me, I choose to let the issue die and enjoy the rest of our lunch together. To my surprise, Bri doesn't seem so uptight anymore. I actually allow myself to believe that maybe some of her anxiety had been over the gift, but I'm not fooling myself.

When we reach the store again, I surprise Bri by going inside with her. She gives me a bewildered look as I walk behind her to the back office, but I just smile and wink which makes her blush.

Adorable.

"You know," I lean against the doorframe to her office as she moves to her desk. "That gift was really cute." I've got the little Bible tucked into my breast pocket, right over my heart. I know, it's cheesy, but … listen … when you're in love, you do stupid, cheesy things.

Brianna glances up as she arranges some files. "I bought it last night."

"Is there a special reason why?"

"Not particularly." She looks over at me again when I cross my arms over my chest. "Should there be a particular reason why?"

I lay a hand over my chest like I've been hurt. "Bri, you wound me."

"I'm so confused," she admits.

"My birthday is in three days. Don't tell me you've forgotten."

Her eyes widen and she freezes in place, letting me know that she had in fact forgotten. I'm not offended, it's been quite a while and I've never been big on birthdays anyway. Still, I'm not going to pass up the chance to sneak another gift out of Bri.

"I'm so sorry!" she gushes. "I've still got time to buy you something else!"

I chuckle, pushing off the wall to cross the room to her. "There's only one thing I want from you, Bri."

She pauses, blinking slowly. "What is it? I'll buy it." Her voice is a whisper.

"It can't be bought."

She tucks a curl behind her ear. It's the cutest thing she's ever done.

"What is it?" she asks again.

I lean down, and she rises on her tiptoes to meet me—but I kiss her forehead instead of her lips. I can tell she's surprised by the way she stiffens at the contact, but I wrap my arms around her before she can pull away and get angry.

"I want your forgiveness," I say in her ear.

Brianna relaxes into my arms. "Bobby..."

"I came back to clear my name. To make sure you were safe. I even entertained the idea of us getting back together. But underneath it all, I just wanted you to forgive me, Bri."

She leans back and stares at me, her brown eyes filled with emotion. "Bobby, I forgave you weeks ago. Even before you told me everything about my father and brother. I just never had the chance to tell you."

She had already forgiven me. Without even knowing the truth. Without having an explanation for my absence or a justification for what'd happened to her. Brianna had decided on her own that she didn't care. That I was worth a second chance.

My hand cups the back of her head as I kiss her. It's such a natural, normal exchange. Like her lips were made to be kissed—only by me. I'm such a kid right now, with my eyes closed and my heart pounding. We aren't even having a knockdown make out session, tearing at each other's clothes. We're just kissing. Two people, two souls, entwined. And it's the most perfect, most blissful moment of my life.

"I love you," I whisper when she pulls away for air.

Briana gasps and just stares up at me.

Oops... Was that too much? Too soon?

I can't read the expression on her face; it's perfectly blank. Like Bri has no idea how to react. But before she can even begin to formulate a response, someone behind us clears their throat and we both jerk away from each other.

Lyla stands in the open doorway, blinking at us like she isn't sure if she's in trouble or not. "I'm sorry," she starts, but Brianna cuts her off.

"What are you doing here?" she snaps, marching over to the door.

"I just got back from my lunch break—"

"And you couldn't knock?" She's yelling now, startling both me and Lyla.

"Bri, calm down," I say, but she turns on me and the look

199

on her face immediately hushes me.

"Get back to work," she orders Lyla, and then slams the door in her face.

For a few moments, neither one of us speaks. I honestly don't know what to say. Brianna paces the room with her arms folded over her chest, shaking her head and muttering to herself. Then she stops and leans over her desk, heaving out a sigh like she's in physical pain.

"Brianna—"

"*Don't*," she snaps. "Just don't say anything."

"I don't understand."

"She saw us!" Brianna whirls around to face me, mist gathering in her eyes. "She saw us kissing."

I chuckle. Slide my hands into my pockets. "So what? She was going to find out about us soon enough."

Brianna shakes her head, pressing the back of her hand to her mouth.

That's when it hits me.

"Bri," I say slowly, "she was going to find out about us, right?"

"I ... I don't know."

"You don't know."

"She's my assistant."

"Okay, and?"

"And how would it look if I told her I was dating my security guard?"

I step back like I've been slapped. I *feel* like I've been slapped. After all this... after everything Brianna and I have been through, the thing that stops her from pursuing the very real love between us isn't my past or the rumors chasing me down—it isn't even her faith.

It's my job.

I know what I am. I know how much money Brianna makes and how much money I don't make. What I didn't know was that any of that mattered to Bri.

I shake my head as I stare at her, for the first time wondering who this woman truly is. "Was there ever a chance for me, Bri?"

"Bobby," she sighs.

I hold my hand up because that's all the answer I need. "You know what? I shouldn't even be surprised. You've always been a princess."

The word stabs her in the heart, I know it does from the way she pales and leans against her desk to stable herself. *Princess* was a nickname I'd given her because she had been so prissy and spoiled when I'd met her. How could she not be, growing up as the only daughter to a billionaire. But even though I'd known she was a diva; I'd never used the word in a derogatory manner. Not until now.

I turn toward the door.

"Wait—" Brianna calls. "Bobby, please. It's not how you think."

I rip open the door. "I've got to get back to work, Miss Gem. If you don't mind."

19

It wasn't like that. I swear it wasn't. I don't care about Bobby's job or how much money he makes. But I know that everyone else around me will care, so I wanted to tell my friends and family about our relationship in my own time, in my own way.

But I never got the chance to explain that to Bobby. Never got to clear the air. To tell him that he was wrong and that I didn't care about money at all. I know I've always been a spoiled princess to him, but when he said it in my office, I knew he meant it differently. I knew it was supposed to be an insult, and it stung just like one. But instead of chasing after Bobby and trying to explain things, I decide to let him go.

Space is what we need. After my shift, I'll close up the shop and talk to him as we walk home. That should be enough time for him to cool down and hear me out.

Except none of that ever happens.

When I walk out of my office hours later, waving goodbye to Lyla who scurries off like a frightened mouse, I find Hans standing in his usual corner of the store.

My heart stops.

"Good evening, Miss Gem," Hans says cheerily.

I offer my best version of a smile and walk over to him. "When did you get here?"

"This afternoon."

"Where's Bobby?"

He pauses, its minute, the slightest hesitation right before he speaks. But I catch it, and I immediately know something's up. That I'm not going to like whatever cockamamie story he's about to feed me.

"Bobby called in sick. I came over to cover for him."

I place a hand on my hip. "Sick?"

He nods. "I'm sure he'll be better tomorrow."

I have half a mind to pull out my phone and call Bobby right now, but the last thing I want to do is cause a scene in front of Hans. I don't know how much he knows about my relationship with Bobby, but the strangely anxious look on his face tells me he knows enough. Somehow, I'm certain if he had to pick sides, he wouldn't pick mine. He's already covering for Bobby with that 'called in sick' story we both know is a lie. The best I can do is give him some space and try his cell later.

Hans and I walk home without saying a word to each other. It's a heavy sort of silence that feels more like a straight jacket than a gentle blanket of quiet. I know Hans isn't offended, he hasn't been working for me as long as Bobby, but he's been around long enough to pick up on my moods. I appreciate his professionalism, the fact that he isn't bothered by our lack of conversation. That he doesn't feel the need to pry or ask questions. I'm glad I don't have to explain to him what's going on with Bobby, and I'm glad he doesn't expect me to do anything beyond the boundaries of our contract.

When we reach my apartment, he stands sentinel outside without even needing the direction. There is no question of whether I want him to come in, enjoy some evening coffee, have a snack. Hans does his duty and I do mine.

Without Bobby to make me any food, I contemplate ordering takeout as I change into a pair of sweatpants and an oversized t-shirt. As I drag my laundry basket to the washer, I pause and feel my cheeks burn with embarrassment. Bobby's clothes are still in the wash, I'd tossed them in after he used my bathroom to shower and change his clothes. I probably shouldn't have machine-washed a tux, but I hadn't thought about it and Bobby hadn't stopped me.

I shrug and grab the damp clothes, tossing them into the dryer without hesitation. They're already ruined, can't get much worse than a round in the dryer.

Still... my concerns have very little to do with the nice clothes I carelessly threw into the wash. I'm worried about the man who owns those clothes. A quick glance at my phone sends me into further despair. No missed calls or texts.

I swallow my pride and dial his number. It doesn't even ring, just goes straight to voicemail. There's a lump in my throat now, but I won't let it reduce me to tears. I've cried over Bobby more times than I care to admit. I won't do it now.

He'll come around, I tell myself. I love Bobby and I know he loves me—he just said he did right before he stormed out and called in 'sick.' This is our first real fight as a couple, that's all.

Except, I'm not sure we are a couple anymore. And if we aren't, I know it's because of me. I know it's all my fault. But there's a lot more on the table right now than Bobby's bruised ego and my high standards. We're dealing with my murderous brother and all his scheming. Bobby and I need to be working together, especially with the deal I've struck with Greyson hanging over my head.

I have a week to do something. To gather the information I need to get my brother arrested for the crimes I know he's committed. But I can't do that without Bobby, and Bobby has no idea we're on a timeline now.

I should have told him. I should have come clean and let him in on the plans I made without him, but I'd chickened out at the last second and changed the subject.

At the time, I'd been glad Bobby hadn't pressed the issue. It was better for us to smile and enjoy the peaceful moment between us, exchanging gifts like a cute couple out for lunch. But now I see the stupidity of my cowardice.

If I can't get in touch with Bobby soon, we might be in deep trouble.

I heave a sigh as I move into the kitchen and glare at my refrigerator. I hate cooking, but I especially hate it now because it just reminds me of Bobby and all the times he would make my favorite foods.

What happens if I can't contact him?

I don't want to make room in my head for the fearful

thought but it's there before I can block it. My only solace is the fact that Bobby knows there's a bigger picture here. He knows who Greyson is and what he's after. He might be angry with me, and we may not get over this bump as quickly as I'd like us to, but he isn't going to abandon me. Not again. Not like this.

"He'll be back," I whisper, taking out ingredients for spaghetti.

I make my dinner in silence and sit down to eat at the kitchen bar. It tastes good, but I find no enjoyment in the food. It's just sustenance right now, something I've got to shove down to survive.

20

I stormed out of Brianna's office well aware that I was overreacting, but I didn't care. I was pissed and I was sick and tired of being taken advantage of. I got screwed over by Colonel Gem and Greyson. I got screwed over by my own background—even that thug in the alley six years ago played a part in screwing me over. And now, for the first time in a very long time, things seem to be working out in my favor, but Brianna has to go and ruin it.

She's embarrassed of me.

The thought makes my ears burn red and my cheeks flush. I haven't felt so stupid in years.

Don't get me wrong, I know—deep down—I truly believe Brianna doesn't really care about how much money I make. But I'm still upset. I'm angry because her hesitation about our relationship reminded me of everything everyone used to say when we were kids.

I have enough reminders of who I am and what I've done. I never expected any of them to come from Bri.

I've been poor all my life. Contrary to what your dirty little mafia novels like to tell you, not every mafia family is filthy rich. My family was broke *because* of the mafia.

My father could have gotten good money by doing jobs for the Jägermeister, but after getting arrested during a job gone wrong and spending three years in prison, he wanted to stay as far away from the Hunting Grounds as possible. As an adult who's been to prison, I don't blame him for wanting to live a good, clean life. But as a kid—a hungry, dirt-stained kid—I only resented him for his decision.

We desperately needed the money Uwe Jäger could have given us, but my father was a proud man who wanted to earn an honest living. He tried his best to keep his family away from the German mafia. But that made it difficult for him to find clean work.

Despite the fact that we weren't closely tied to the Hunting Grounds, no one wanted to hire a man with a German last name during the mafia's hay day. And after the defunding, it was still hard for him to get work with his record and our family's history hanging over our heads.

But no matter how much money my family had, or didn't have, it never came between Brianna and me. She knew who I was. Knew I was living with my aunt and uncle, not in the trashy apartment I'd grown up in. That place was nothing more than a dinky little cave tucked into the projects of New York.

It had two bedrooms—one for my parents and one I shared with my brother for my entire life. There were holes in the walls and two pots in the kitchen which my mother used to cook everything. On good days, we had meat and potatoes, on bad days she'd throw whatever she could find into a pot of water and boil it down.

We called it *Everything Soup*—ground beef a day away from spoiling, the last few squirts of ketchup from a near empty bottle, salt, pepper, half a jar of olives, some questionable-looking carrots partly shriveled and hidden behind the half-empty carton of 2 percent milk, which was also thrown into the pot. We would top it off with the leftover box of expired macaroni noodles that was *always* in the cupboard. And then we'd eat.

It tasted like crap, and I hated every spoonful, but it was food and I was hungry. And most nights there was nothing else, so there you go. Brianna's parents were right. I was trailer trash. I wasn't good enough for her. But she had never believed that herself. Not until now.

I saw it in her eyes, the tiniest flicker of panic at the very thought of Lyla finding out that Princess Gem was banging her security guard. Pardon my vulgarity, no, we are not *banging* each other. But we were tangled up in her office and Lyla, admittedly, saw more than she should have. But still… It was nothing Bri should have been ashamed of.

Her words ring in my ears as I march down the street, *what will she think of me dating my security guard?* I don't know, Bri, she'll think you're a fortunate woman who found a man that's madly in love with you. *Or* she'll think you can do better than the hired help.

I grunt as I round a corner, walking so hard I'm practically stomping down the street. A few people shoot me mildly curious looks, but I don't give a crap about them right now.

Normally, I try hard not to stand out in crowds. I make it my business to blend in so I can do my job well. But I'm not even sure I want this job anymore. I'm not sure how I'm supposed to handle being around Bri after that argument.

But there's so much more at stake besides my pride. I'm so angry and embarrassed I could scream and punch something, set loose the anger I've been keeping at bay since I got out of prison. I had to do things in there that no man should ever experience. I had to fight for my life, had to tuck away my humanity to complete the jobs assigned to me.

I had ice in my veins when I was in prison. There was no one I feared but myself because I'd become my own worst enemy. I was the monster they said I'd always been, and when I got out, I vowed I'd never be that man again.

But that's the man I need to be right now. Ice cold, detached, void of all the things that make me weak. Things like love.

Brianna has become a distraction. I'm glad she's forgiven me, I'm glad she cares about my soul, but it's clear there are still things between us that need to be ironed out and I can't afford to be consumed by our drama. Not when there's a crazy diamond jeweler out there who's willing to kill us both just to get what he wants.

I was caught up with Brianna when that car jumped the curb—left with barely a moment to get her out the way. I was caught up with Brianna when Lyla walked into her office and saw us together, any other time, I would have heard her coming the moment she entered the store. But I hadn't been paying attention. I hadn't been doing my job.

"She's throwing me off," I mumble, still marching down the street, and—as if to prove me right—it's at that exact moment that I'm caught off guard again.

I'm walking through a shady alley, cutting corners to get home quicker, when someone comes up from behind. Not only is the alleyway dank and lonely, giving this mysterious assailant a cover, but there's also a curtain of my own distracting emotions that keeps him hidden until the last moment. I never hear any footsteps, never feel anyone's presence until it's too late.

The area to my left darkens a shade as the sun is suddenly blocked by a body. I notice at the very last second, sucking in a gasp when I glance up to see who's invaded my personal space. There's a black blur and then a burning pain in my temple as I'm cracked in the side of the head. Stars burst into my vision and then I'm drifting away, knocked unconscious.

___ .O. ___

When I wake, I hear voices. They're all muffled and tough to make out, like my head is underwater. Pain blooms in my temple and radiates through my entire head, I feel it throbbing in my forehead, I feel it knocking against the very top of my head. There's pain everywhere.

I shift my feet and realize I'm tied up, a rope around my

ankles and one around my wrists, bound behind my back. I'm lying on my side on cold concrete. The lighting in the room is fake, bright fluorescent bulbs that flicker every few seconds.

Now the fog is clearing. The voices are still muffled, but I'm coherent enough to pick up the echoey sound I can only relate to wide, open spaces. That, paired with the concrete ground and the cheap fluorescent lights lets me know I'm in a warehouse. And as I blink my aching eyes and glance blearily around the room, I notice three massive safes—each the size of a shed—and I know whose warehouse I'm in.

I groan as I roll over, trying to sit up. The voices stop, replaced by the sound of footsteps growing nearer.

"He's up," someone says, then I'm dragged to my knees and my head is yanked back by my hair.

I'm sure I cry out in pain, but the sound is cut off as I'm punched hard in the jaw. The hit rocks me—the room sways as my head lolls to the side. Gravity seems to suspend for a moment as I fight the darkness edging my vision. I can't pass out again. Not here. Not now. I need to look these men in their faces and spew my hatred. It's the least I can do before they kill me.

I grunt as I lift my head, blinking back the sweat that's running down my face. There are six people in the room, well-dressed men as tall and muscular as me. Security guards, all except one.

My eyes land on Greyson Gem and ignite with fire. If only I could burn him alive with just a look...

He smiles and walks toward me, pulling up the legs of his

pants before squatting in front of me. "Bobby boy."

I spit a glob of blood at his foot which earns me another brutal blow to the face from the guard standing next to me.

"Why?" I grind out.

Greyson sighs. "You let my sister get to you." He pokes me in the chest. "I told you to seduce her and tell her to hand the store over to me. But it sounds like the exact opposite happened."

I shake my head. "I have no idea what you're talking about."

Greyson glances at the guard and he punches me again. I set loose a string of curses, one of which includes an insult about Greyson's mother—then I'm punched again, and I have to bite my tongue to keep myself conscious. The sharp pain and the coppery twang of blood in my mouth keeps me awake. I can't take many more hits. The guy beside me isn't letting up, and there are four other guys standing behind Greyson, all ready to stomp me into the ground at his command.

I glare at them as I suck for breath, trying to breathe around my broken nose. They're all men I've never seen before, but I want to memorize their faces. I can't do anything to them now, but if I ever make it out of here, I'm going to hunt every last one of them down. And if they do kill me, I'll hunt them down in Hell.

But my heart stops as I glance at the last security guard. I recognize him. Average sized guy with dark hair, streaks of grey going through it to tell everyone his age. He works for Stronghold Inc. There's no way to tell if he's truly on Greyson's side or if he's just a hired guard out on contract, just like me.

Grey's voice draws my attention from the guard back to him. "Don't lie to me, Bobby boy."

I hate that nickname.

"You've been talking to Brianna."

I give him a slow blink, partly because my eye is nearly swollen shut, but also because I'm trying to figure out how on Earth he could possibly know that I've told Brianna everything.

Thanks to his insatiable desire to be right about everything, Greyson very kindly explains how he came across this wonderful information. "She confronted me," he says, voice growing hard. "Actually tried to offer me an ultimatum—your freedom and her safety in exchange for the business." Greyson leans closer. I can smell the mint on his breath as he speaks. "Did you really think I'd give you two a week to scheme behind my back?"

My eyes widen, which sort of hurts.

Brianna had mentioned that we had a week to gather intel, what she didn't mention was the reason why. I'd gotten distracted by her gift and let the conversation die. I should have pushed for more information. I should have insisted that she tell me what was going on. Then I would have been prepared for this—even if I couldn't have prevented Greyson's betrayal, I could have at least *predicted* it and not ended up bound and beaten bloody.

"Whose idea was it?" Greyson asks. "Which one of you really thought you could saunter into that restaurant and make

214

demands to me?" He rises and glares down at me. "I want to hear you say it."

I have no choice but to cover for her.

"It was my idea," I say slowly.

He chuckles. "I figured. There's no way Bri-Bri could've thought that up on her own, not when she's half crazed and hopped up on her anxiety meds all day." He shakes his head and sighs disappointedly. "She's a nut."

"No, she's not," I growl.

The guard who punched me steps forward but Greyson waves him off. "It doesn't matter. Telling her the truth actually works in my favor. Now that she knows what I'm capable of, she'll not only sign over the business, she'll destroy whatever information she's got on me. If she values her safety."

"She'll never do that," I tell him. "That's the thing about Brianna. She *doesn't* value her safety. She'd rather get stabbed a dozen more times than sign her business over to you."

He laughs at me. "She'll do whatever I tell her to do once she finds your dead body."

My blood runs cold. "Y-You can't just kill me. I have a contract, I have a job—people who will look for me if I go missing."

"You won't be missing. You'll be dead. And no one will care." Greyson pulls a gun from his waistband.

I start to shuffle backwards.

"Grey—"

"You'll be one more dead gangster. The police will thank me for getting rid of you."

"You won't get away with this," I say quickly, desperately. I don't want to die. Not here. Not like this.

I'd never feared death when I was in prison, not after coming so close to it on my first night in jail. But this is different. In prison, I really was just another gangster that no one cared about. But I've changed—my entire life has changed. I'm not a gangster anymore, and I've got people who care about me. People who are worth living for.

Hans, Lyla, my boss at Stronghold Inc. Brianna...

I can't die here.

"They'll arrest you!" I shout madly. At this point, I'm just saying anything I can to stop Greyson as he walks toward me, gun in hand.

He doesn't listen.

"My uncle is Commissioner of NYPD. And even if he weren't, the cops won't touch me when I tell them my men caught you breaking into my warehouse. I was stupid enough to show kindness to a former mobster, showing you my chocolate diamonds just days ago. And you got greedy and tried to break in and steal them. My men caught you, a fight ensued. You died trying to escape." He tsks. "Some men never change. That'll be the story on the news."

It isn't enough to shoot me, Greyson will let me die in shame. Just like he let me take the fall six years ago, ruining my reputation and snatching part of my life away for good. I will always be remembered as a thug who did nothing but lie, cheat, steal, and hurt people.

First, I turned on the Gem Princess. Then I got out of

prison and tried to steal from the Gem Prince. The media will eat that up. The cops won't care. And I'll be dead.

"Brianna won't believe that," I say, still scooting backwards. The guard nearby kicks me hard in the side and I topple over with a groan. My neck strains, muscles spasming in pain, as I tilt my head all the way back to look up at Grey. He's standing over me now, an intimidating figure from this angle.

The light reflects off his glasses, making him look blinded, but he doesn't need to see as he smirks. "I don't care what Brianna believes. In fact, I want her to know the truth about how you died. I want her to know what happens when she defies me."

"Greyson—"

He points the gun at me.

God, help me.

"Greyson!"

He pulls the trigger.

I scream as pain shoots through my chest—piercing my heart. I've been stabbed before. I've been punched, kicked, bitten, and burned. But I've never been shot; prisoners don't have guns and prison guards only carry batons and stun guns. This is the most pain I've ever experienced in my life. It takes my breath away and I sob and roll over, blubbering a string of incoherent words.

I'm not even aware of what language I'm speaking, but I know my lips are moving and words are coming out. I'm in so much pain, the only thing I can truly register is the tear that slips down my cheek. I'm crying. Crying and gasping and yanking at the ropes restraining my hands and feet.

Greyson watches me die. For once, there is no smile on his face. He wears the calmest, most solemn expression I've ever seen. Almost like he's sad to see me go.

I squeeze my eyes shut. I don't want the last thing I see to be him. But I know his voice will be the last one I hear.

"Get rid of the body," he orders. And then I listen to his footsteps fade as he turns to leave.

21

I'm in the middle of selling a diamond necklace when I get the phone call that nearly stops my heart. A number I don't recognize flashes on the screen of my phone, I would have ignored it if the mysterious call hadn't been accompanied by a sudden jolt of black fear that stabbed me in the heart.

Somehow, I just knew I had to answer this call.

So I asked Lyla to finish up with the customers and then I took my phone into my office. I'm glad I made that decision because when the disturbingly chipper nurse tells me my husband's been shot, I scream and drop the phone.

I'm not married, but there is only one man in the expanse of the entire universe who would ever claim to be my husband while he's on his deathbed.

I don't remember grabbing my phone or my purse. I don't remember leaving the store. I only vaguely recall sitting in the back of a cab, and then, miraculously, arriving at the hospital. Hans deals with the folks at the front desk who answer his questions with meek, slightly frightened smiles. He's a terrible sight on a good day, so I understand their hesitation as he looms over the desk, his daunting figure casting a dark shadow over their computers as they type. When they tell us Bobby's floor and room, I walk away without waiting for Hans to catch up.

He meets me by the elevator, long legs easily catching up to mine. I'm average height and plus-sized—most people can catch me without effort.

The elevator ride is the longest thirty-six seconds of my life. I'm *this* close to prying the doors apart and shoving past the old man in front of me when we finally reach our floor. I'm panicking, a familiar anxiety slowly uncurling inside of me, it's claws extending, waiting to strike at my heart at the right moment. I try to kill the creature, take deep breaths as I walk, think of good things—positive things. Things like everything I love about Bobby and why he's got to be okay.

He's tall and strong and beautiful and kind and one of the toughest people I know. Guys like Bobby don't die to gunshot wounds. They can't. He can't.

I'm panting as I round the last corner—that's when Hans grabs my arm. I would snatch it away and scream at him, but I don't want to cause a scene and end up getting tackled by the burly security guard who's eyeing me from his stance by the help desk.

"Leave me alone," I say sharply.

Hans's grip on my arm goes slack but he doesn't let me go. His sudden gentleness startles me into submission, and I find myself turning to face him before I can think to stop. I'm glad

I'm not so focused right now. Because if I had been controlled by the thoughts taking over my mind, I would've turned and dropkicked Hans, then stormed off to find Bobby.

Instead, I very calmly say, "What is it?"

"We don't know what condition Robert is in."

The use of his real name shocks me enough that my mind goes blank, tossing out the thoughts of dropkicking my guard as an emptiness settles into my mind. Distantly, I realize Hans is doing this on purpose. Throwing me off so I'm too distracted to spiral into an anxiety attack or fly off the rails.

The worry over Bobby is still there in full force, but I don't feel like I'm drowning anymore. I don't feel like I'm going to faint.

I press my lips together and nod at Hans. It's just one slow bob of my head, but it's enough for him to understand that I'm somewhat sorry and I'm somewhat focused again. I can handle whatever we find in Bobby's room.

Hans lets go of my arm. "Are you ready?"

I nod again, closing the last few steps to Bobby's door. *God, please let him be okay*, I pray as I twist the knob.

When the door opens enough for me to see inside, I gasp as I find Bobby. He's in bed, his face bruised and purple, his torso wrapped in bandages. He looks like he just got ran over by a truck, but the most startling part isn't his appearance, it's what I see around him—rather, what I *don't* see.

There is no machinery in the room. No beeping electronics, no monitors letting me know that his heart is still beating. Bobby's just lying in bed, flat on his back with the blankets pulled up to his waist. His eyes are closed, and his hair is combed. He looks peaceful.

He looks dead.

"No…" I whisper, stumbling forward. From my peripheral, I see Hans reaching out to stable me, but I keep moving until I'm at Bobby's bed. I climb right in and sit beside him, staring at his face, at his swollen eyes and his busted lip, his cheeks so fat they look stuffed with oranges. He's hardly the man I saw two days ago. Part of me hopes this isn't even him, that there's been some mix up.

"He—he's dead?" I say, looking back at Hans.

His face is stony, a carefully crafted expression that is nothing short of stoic. His mouth is hidden beneath his wild beard, but even if I could see it, I know it wouldn't change anything. Hans's face is so calm, he looks like he could easily be discussing his favorite pizza topping, not the death of his own friend.

"Say something," I plead. "Is he dead?"

Before Hans can answer, the door swings open and a nurse walks inside. He startles when he glances up and sees massive Hans standing like a ghoul in the corner, and me all wet-faced and panicky in the bed.

"Oh! You must be Mrs. Ackard." He smiles at me, then glances at Hans.

"Older cousin," Hans lies—though he *could* be related to Bobby. They're both from the Hunting Grounds, even I know the gang is tight enough that almost everyone is related in some way.

The nurse's smile widens a smidge. "Nice to meet you."

"Please tell me," I sniffle. "Is my husband alive?"

His face wrinkles. "Of course he is!"

I blink at him, then I glance back down at Bobby still lying motionless beside me. "Where's all the equipment?"

The nurse laughs. "I just moved it out. He doesn't need it."

"You sure?" Hans asks. He's staring at Bobby like he's counting the hours he's got left.

"I'm positive," the nurse replies coolly, and—as if on cue—Bobby stirs beside me.

I gasp and lean down, gently kissing his cheek. He groans painfully, eyes peeling back as he wakes from his very stiff slumber. I slept beside Bobby a few times in high school, and he's never been this still. Neither of us are very pleasant sleepers, always fighting for the blankets and rolling over every twelve minutes. One night he slept over, I woke up with no covers, laying horizontally across the bed—on top of Bobby. He was loudly snoring without a problem.

"Bobby?" I say, peering into his red eyes.

He lets out another groan, and then sighs deeply. "Hey, Princess."

"What happened?"

"He was shot," the nurse says. "And beaten pretty badly."

"And you're positive he doesn't need anything?" Hans asks again.

The nurse laughs, but I understand Hans's concern. Bobby looks terrible. He used to get into fights quite a bit throughout high school. Elitists would say something about him being poor, jerks would say something about him being mafia, even a few racists had issues with a White kid dating a Black girl. There was a problem every other week. Bobby never had a break, but he also never backed down.

He'd get into fights, get jumped, and even had a few all-out brawls—our friends versus whatever group of spoiled rich brats who had a point to prove. Black eyes, bruises, and scars were a regular thing when we were teenagers. But Bobby's never looked this bad before, and he's certainly never been *shot*.

"Most of the damage was to his face and torso," the nurse reports. "The worst of it was a broken nose and a few bruised ribs."

"But he was shot," I reiterate.

The nurse smiles, lifting a plastic baggy I notice for the first time. A miniature book is inside, one that I recognize. "I came back to give this to Mr. Ackard."

Since Bobby is barely conscious, I reach out and take the bag, my eyes watering at the sight. It's the pocket Bible I bought. The same little Book that'd put a smile on Bobby's face as he'd tucked it into his breast pocket. Right over his heart.

I glance down at Bobby to find that he's managed to form a serious expression on his battered face. His gaze isn't bleary or unfocused anymore, he's looking directly at me.

"He saved me," he says. And I know exactly what he means. There's a hole in the middle of the Bible, likely where the bullet had been lodged.

"I told you," the nurse says kindly, "he doesn't need

anything except aspirin."

I laugh. Laugh so hard that tears begin to stream down my face. I'm so happy Bobby's okay, so happy that the worst hasn't happened. But I'm most excited because I know God played a part in this. I don't have all the details. I have no idea what Bobby's been through the last few days, but I know God was with Him. And I know Bobby knows that too.

I stay at the hospital as long as I can the first day. Mostly, Bobby sleeps, only waking long enough to take more pain pills, limp to the bathroom, and slurp tepid soup. We don't really talk, but I'm not upset. The silence is actually comforting in its own way.

Bobby and I don't really need words. In the aftermath of whatever nightmare he's gone through, the problems we had with each other have melted away. In the brief moments of Bobby's consciousness, we're both just happy to have each other. There's a bigger problem outside the walls of this hospital, a monster waiting to strike again. Even though I have no details on what happened, I know my brother is somehow involved.

It takes another day for the doctors to clear Bobby for release. He leans against me as we walk out of the hospital, though I'm sure Hans would be better support. Neither of us wants to be apart for more than a few seconds. We hold hands while Hans drives us back to my apartment, he had men from

Stronghold Inc. sweep it for bugs and such while I was with Bobby at the hospital. We don't trust anyone anymore, and once Bobby sits down and tells me what happened, it's easy to understand why.

Hans is there, standing by the door like a statue as Bobby explains how he was kidnapped and beaten by men under Greyson's order. My brother is a madman, and the only reason he hasn't come for me yet is because I've hardly been home. I've let Lyla run the shop since I first got the call about my 'husband' being in the hospital. Greyson called my cellphone only once. I didn't answer.

"He probably knows I'm still alive by now," Bobby says.

"Even though you didn't file a police report?" I ask.

He shakes his head. The police had come to take a statement, considering he'd been shot, but when Bobby woke up in the hospital, he truly had no idea how he'd gotten there so he told them he couldn't remember much and they left him alone. NYPD has 8 million people to deal with, a beaten-up former gangster who doesn't want to talk is the least of their worries.

It was honestly smart to derail the police, considering Greyson has our uncle doing dirty work for him. There's no telling which side of the law any officer is really on.

"What will you do now?" Hans asks. He folds his arms over his big chest and waits patiently for an answer. His face is still stony but there is an undeniable edge to his voice as he says, "I hope you plan to retaliate."

Bobby nods then winces. "I do. But not in the way you're

thinking."

Hans grunts and mutters something in German. Bobby glares at him and doesn't offer to translate.

"I don't need to retaliate through violence," he explains. "I can get solid evidence that will put Greyson behind bars."

"How?" I ask.

He reaches for my hand, and I take it willingly. We're sitting on the sofa in my living room, Bobby's big body takes up over half of it, but I don't mind. I'm just glad to see him conscious and relatively okay. His face still has bad bruises, and he can't talk much without stopping to wince or clutch at his ribs, but he's alive.

"I have to talk to some folks at work," Bobby tells me. "They'll be able to help."

Hans says something else in German.

Bobby sighs and then responds in the same tongue.

I get angry.

"Guys, don't talk like I'm not in the room. That's rude."

Hans turns and walks out of the apartment without another word, making me turn my glare to Bobby. "What's going on?"

"Hans wants to draw blood."

"And you don't."

He shakes his head. I feel his grip on my hand tightening, I'm not sure if its subconscious or not.

"Bri, if things go our way, it could get ugly. Greyson will go to jail, but we'll both probably be dragged through the media."

I don't care. I grew up as the only daughter to a billionaire. I'm used to people sticking their noses in my business. Unfortunately, so is Bobby. People have always been in his business, for good or bad reasons. But this will be different. We'll be going after my own family.

Bobby senses my hesitation and wraps his arm around my shoulders. I try not to lean into him too much, so I won't cause him any pain, but he grits his teeth and pulls me close anyway.

He exhales into my hair, his breath blowing a curl out of place. "We have to make a decision."

I know I should take my time and think about this, consider my future and the future of my business. What this will do to my relationship with my parents. But the truth is that the answer comes to me naturally, without thought or uncertainty.

"Do it, Bobby. Whatever you need to."

He kisses the top of my head. "Brianna—"

"He tried to *kill* you," I say sharply. "If it weren't for God, you'd be dead."

"I can't argue with that."

I lean away to look him in the face. This is the closest he's ever come to even acknowledging that there is a God. My shock must be written all over my face because Bobby smiles and shrugs sheepishly. He pulls out the pocket Bible still tucked in its plastic baggy; a hole burned into the center.

"God's Word literally saved my life," Bobby says, staring at the Bible. "If that's not a wakeup call to get myself together, then I don't know what is."

I try to blink away my tears as I watch him stare at the battered Book.

He chuckles. "Best birthday gift ever."

I'd almost forgotten about his birthday! He'd spent it in the hospital, bruised and beaten, but alive. Maybe he's right, despite what he's gone through, this is the best gift he's ever gotten. Nothing can compare to the joy and peace that comes with the presence of God in your life.

The contemplative look on Bobby's face draws a question out of me. "So, what are you saying?" I ask him slowly.

He grins, though it pains him. "I'm ready to do right by God. Like, I'm *really* ready."

I believe him. He was kidnapped, beaten, and shot in the heart. And with Greyson still on the loose, we could both die at any given moment. What he's experienced is enough to bring anyone to salvation. I hate to say it, but I'm glad this has happened. I hate the pain Bobby went through, but it's nothing compared to what he's about to gain.

I'm sure there's a scripture for that—*these light afflictions…*

22

I spend another two days sleeping on Brianna's couch. For once, she doesn't complain about me bumming on her sofa, in fact, I have to tell her to leave me alone every time she comes out to check on me. I'm bruised and tired and full of anger, but I'm not dying. I want Bri to get her sleep and focus on herself right now. I promised her I'd get the evidence we need and I'm going to come through on that.

"Do you trust me, Bri?" I ask her when she catches me dressing myself to go out this morning. She runs over and tries to force me back to bed, swearing I need more time to heal. Most of the bruises on my face are better now, fading from deep purple to a flaming red. I look like I've been violently slapped rather than curb stomped by guys the size of football players. My ribs still hurt like a mother.

Brianna sucks in a long breath and blows it out slowly, her cheeks fat and puffed like a petulant child's. "Of course I trust you."

"Then let me do this, babe."

She bites her lip and gives me a little grin at the sound of the pet name. If I didn't feel like I was just dropped off the top of her apartment complex, I would pull her close and kiss her until she couldn't breathe. But *I* can barely breathe with my bruised ribs aching in my chest.

I settle for patting her shoulder in a friendly manner.

Brianna frowns. "That's quite a romantic gesture."

"Clean and wholesome." I wink.

She snorts. "Good ol' Christian romance."

I don't care about my ribs anymore. I snake an arm around her waist and kiss her deeply, murmuring as I pull away, "Let's get married, babe."

She snaps her head up at me. There is surprise on her face, but also mischief and desire and everything else I used to see in her eyes when were restless teens. But now we aren't sneaking out, dodging her parents and all her godly little rules. We're adults trying to navigate our feelings and keep ourselves from crossing a line we both promised we wouldn't anymore.

This is not new to me. I went to church with Bri throughout high school, even though I never really cared for her faith. But things are different now, I have a chance to start over and take things seriously. And I don't mind doing it. I told Brianna I was ready to do right by God, and I meant it. The first thing I want to do is treat her the way she's meant to be treated.

Brianna smiles at me, her eyes filled with emotions. "Are you serious?"

I nod silently.

"Don't play games with me."

"I'm not playing." I chuckle, which probably makes it seem like I *am* playing games, but Bri knows me well enough to tell when I'm laughing nervously versus genuinely. It dawns on me then that I *am* nervous. Like, really freaking nervous.

I have no ring. I have a crap job and a crappier reputation. I look half dead and I haven't showered in two days. And, somehow, I've decided this is the perfect moment to propose to the woman I love.

Getting down on one knee would probably make this more romantic. But it would also suck so bad with how sore I am. I almost do it, but my aching ribs are all like *no, don't,* so I stay upright and pull Brianna toward me again. She's still high off her girly emotions, too distracted to care if I'm being traditional or not.

I steal a kiss from her lips, smiling as she giggles into my mouth.

"Marry me, babe," I say in a low voice.

She wraps her arms around my neck. "Really?"

"Really."

Brianna pauses, her face shifting into a more serious expression. "Before I answer, I want you to know I don't care about how much money you make."

"I know."

"What happened in my office—"

"Don't worry about it," I tell her quickly. "I overreacted."

"I'm sorry anyway."

I kiss her. "Please just tell me you'll marry me."

232

Brianna laughs. "Of course I'll marry you."

___ .O. ___

I leave Brianna's apartment with enough pep in my step to cover the limp I've got. I'm still sore, but I'm well enough to walk around. Well enough to get this done.

Hans stayed to watch over Bri while I'm gone, he's the only man I trust in this city right now. Everyone else is questionable, but I know a few men who'll see things clearly when I explain the situation.

I go to the headquarters of Stronghold Inc., taking a cab all the way to the Bronx so I can talk to my boss face to face. He's not a bad guy at all, in fact, he's been nothing but good to me since he took me in. I've never seen the guy get angry or even stern, but his kind demeanor doesn't fool me. I know he's got a past as dark as mine. I know Stronghold Inc. was built by former mafia. I know he'll know exactly what to do about this whole mess. I just hope his advice won't be as bloody as Hans's.

There's music thumping through all of Stronghold Inc. I can hear the deep bass drifting through the facility, swelling in the halls, nearly shaking the walls. It's always like this in here, dim lighting, people lazily walking through the foyer like it's a casual club and not an elite security force. That's what happens when an entire empire of businesses is built by a group of tightknit friends who all happen to be former mobsters.

The whole place is made of concrete, built like a dark

fortress—or a stronghold. The walls are cracked and cement-grey, crumbles of concrete drift to the floor and coat everything in gritty dust. The air always smells of chalk and earth. The décor is equally as bland, steel desks and metal chairs to match. It gives the base a harsh look, like walking back into prison.

I've never felt out of place in Stronghold Inc., never felt judged, never felt like I didn't belong. Everyone here has as many tattoos as me, as many scars, as many nightmares. There are even some who consider me a lightweight, like Hans who was in the real German mafia while it was in its prime. And also like my boss, the man who built this place with his wife—a former mafia princess.

I'm searching for my boss when I turn the corner into one of the offices, but I find one of my closest friends instead.

"White Boy Rob!" Brandon says as I enter the room. It's a name I earned back in high school, being the only White kid in Brianna's group of friends. It started as an insult but eventually molded into a nickname that makes me grin every time I hear it.

"What up, B." I slap him up, trying not to wince when he claps me on the back with his big meaty hand. Brandon's a big guy, tall and handsome with dark brown skin stretched taut over large muscles. He's ripped enough to make me blush.

"Where've you been?" he asks me, taking a closer look at my face.

I shrug. "Trouble."

"Sheesh, White Boy, someone messed you up good."

I roll my eyes. "Thanks, B."

He grins and it's almost pretty, except that I know Brandon's smile hides fangs. He's one of the most ruthless guys I know. Been working for the Stronghold since he was a teenager. He's one of the few kids I kept in touch with after moving to live with my aunt in Manhattan—even Brianna knows him from the days when he would crash our parties and claim our friends as his own.

Brandon grew up in the streets just like me, but *unlike* me, he really was in a gang as a kid. That's why he's so loyal to the Stronghold, it's the only place that could offer him a decent job with his sordid background. But even though he's here, I still don't believe he's totally done with the dark side of New York. The cops might have gotten rid of the five famous gangs of the city, but there are still criminals operating in secret. I'd bet good money Brandon's one of them.

His little cousin sitting in the corner of the room is proof that something's up.

"Babysitting?" I jerk my chin at the kid, unsure how much B is willing to discuss in front of him. He's sitting in a chair against the wall of the small office, wearing a school uniform even though it's the weekend. Honey-toned skin and dark wavy hair, he's a cute teenager who I'm sure would rather be out with a girl than locked up here, but I don't comment on that.

Brandon rolls his eyes. "His dad sent him up from California."

"Things bad out there?"

"Things are bad everywhere."

I blink at the kid; he's got his nose in a book that's good enough to keep him from even acknowledging my presence. I'm not offended by his aloofness; I already know who he is, no introduction is necessary.

His name is Vito Gerardo. A kid Brandon swears is distant family, a little cousin he babysits from time to time, but I know better. I heard whispers while I was in prison. I know about the underground gangs of New York, forces coming together to retake the city. It's a new generation of thugs who sat back and watched the chaos that happened with the defunding and all the madness that followed years ago. They have learned from the mistakes of their elders, and they don't plan to repeat them.

They want to capture New York again, but not through violence and anarchy like their forefathers. They'll do it through diplomacy—charm the public and swindle the politicians. They will infiltrate the police force, take over office, and rule from the inside out.

The mafia will rise again, slowly, quietly. But they won't cause the Big Apple to rot, they'll nurture it. Take it from an angry city and turn it into a flourishing kingdom.

Vito Gerardo will rule that kingdom when he's older. That's why he's here now, Brandon's grooming him—the Prince of the City.

B can deny all he wants, say the kid is family visiting from across the county, but he isn't fooling me. I heard of the Gerardos when I was locked up, and even if I hadn't, I've been around mafioso enough to know one when I see one. Vito comes from a dangerous line. I can tell from just looking at him.

But that's none of my business. Vito's just a kid right now, no older than fifteen or sixteen. He's still got some time before he can cause any real damage. Hopefully he'll lose interest and stay in California before he's old enough to take over his father's empire. Maybe Brandon will come to his senses and see how insane it is to groom a child to rule a gang.

Knowing B, he'll probably try to steal the prince's crown for himself. He's always loved the shadows. I know he's itching for the day the mafia rises again. Meanwhile, I've been trying all my life to get away from it. And I've finally found my chance.

"Where's the boss?" I ask B.

He frowns. "He's been locked in his office. Something crazy went down a few days ago, don't know what."

I do.

"I'll go see him," I say, turning away.

Brandon shouts a goodbye over my shoulder. As I walk out the door, Vito doesn't move. He's still staring into his book, but I don't miss the very discrete look he shoots me. It's a sideways glance, his stony eyes peeling from his book for half a second.

If I hadn't been looking right at him, I would've missed it.

As promised, my boss is in his office. I can hear his voice as I approach, talking to someone in hushed, angry-sounding tones. When I knock, the voices stop, and I clear my throat.

"It's Robert," I announce.

The door swings open, revealing my boss and a man I instantly recognize. He's got the same dark hair I remember. The same slate grey eyes. The same blank look on his face, but his expression changes when he recognizes me.

I go from calm to homicidal in an instant.

"You!" I shout, rushing into the office.

My boss steps in front of me, using all of his weight to hold me back. I'm a tall guy, 6'4 and 260 pounds of lean muscle, but my boss is just as big and years older with much more experience in fighting angry thugs like me.

I am quickly reminded of his might and strength as he twists my sore body into a headlock and says into my ear, "Cool it, Rob. Eike is one of us, you know that."

"He didn't look like one of us when he stood there and watched me get shot!" I snarl.

I feel my boss's grip loosen.

"You were there?" he says to Eike who's standing there watching us with wide eyes.

I groan, ribs screaming fire through my chest. "Let me go. I'm calm."

My boss drops me and the three of us stand there staring at each other. I glance between the two men, Eike Brandt, a former Hunter from the German mafia. He's older than me, near his forties, with a streak of grey through his dark hair and a deep set of crow's feet around his eyes. He reminds me of a college professor, but in a way that makes me remember everything I hated about school.

I've seen Eike around here before, he's one of the originals. A guy who was here with my boss when he started Stronghold Inc., along with Hans and a few others.

"Douglass," Eike says to my boss. The sound of his name draws his attention, and he stands to his full height.

Douglass Solomon opened Stronghold Inc. right after the fall of the mafia. It was built on gang money and run by former gangsters, one of many businesses that's gotten famous for its ties to the mafia. Douglass was a member of the gang known as the Willis Stronghold, but at age 16 he was kidnapped by Hunters from the German mafia and forced to join their ranks.

He served as a grunt at the bottom of the barrel, branded with a bullseye to let other gangsters know he belonged to the Hunting Grounds. The mark was burned onto the back of his left hand, I stare at it as he moves to pour himself a drink at the display in the corner.

Despite being kidnapped and forced to work as a grunt in another gang, Douglass didn't break. He rose through the ranks of the Hunting Grounds and became the personal guard and most trusted ally of Amory Jäger himself. When the mafia fell, Douglass married Nona Willis, granddaughter to the boss of the Stronghold—a mafia princess through and through.

Together, they started Stronghold Inc., uniting the leftover thugs of the Hunting Grounds and the Stronghold without shedding any blood. It's the reason Hans loves this place, why I was able to find a job here and fit in so easily, and why Eike Brandt, a former Hunter, is standing in my boss's office calling him by his first name like they're old friends.

They *are* old friends. Eike was married to one of Amory Jäger's cousins back in the day. He worked side by side with Douglass right up until the cops retook the city. That's why I'm so confused as to why Eike stood across the room and watched in silence while I was beaten to a pulp.

"You're a traitor," I say to him.

Eike shakes his head. "I was on a job. Just like you. I had no idea what that guy was gonna do to you."

"And when you found out, you didn't try to stop it."

"I was outnumbered. There was nothing I could do, and you know it."

"That's your excuse?" I take a step closer but my boss eyes me from across the room and I stay put. I'm itching to wrap my hands around Eike's throat, but I know Douglass will likely wrap his around mine if I do that.

He's stubborn about us all respecting each other. *The rest of the world is ready to fight, in here, we work together*—that's what he's always told me in his deep bass of a voice. There's a quiet strength to Douglass, a surety in his demeanor that leaves no question about his authority. While he's normally calm and kind, I have no doubt he'll snap my neck if he needs to. I see his ferocity caged behind his relaxed expression, the way his dark brown skin folds and forms the planes of his face, giving him a look of focus. Controlled power.

Douglass's words work their way into my head as I try to calm down. *In here, we work together.* My chest is still burning flames, but I cling to my boss's commitment and loyalty as a reminder that I won't have to suffer this pain again, a reminder that someone's got my back. It's easy to calm down when you know you've got allies in the room—that, and the fact that Douglass is still glaring at me like he wants to tackle me to the floor.

I swallow. "I'm guessing you know what happened, boss?"

He nods. "Eike filled me in after he dropped you off at the hospital."

My head whips in his direction. "You took me to the hospital?" I had no idea how I wound up there. I was just grateful God had saved me.

Eike nods. "After Greyson shot you, I volunteered to take care of your body. I took pictures of you and sent them to him like he wanted."

So he could use them to taunt and frighten Brianna.

"And then I hauled you into the back of my truck. That's when you groaned, and I realized you were alive. I changed direction, driving to the hospital instead of the dumpsite."

"Police didn't question you?" I ask.

He shakes his head. "They didn't get the chance. I dropped you off at the doors and left. Came straight here and have been hiding out ever since."

"Hiding out," I repeat.

"Greyson probably knows you're alive by now. Which means it won't take long for him to figure out I helped save you." Eike runs his hand through his hair. "I'm sorry I didn't step up when you wanted. But I did the right thing when it mattered most."

241

The room falls silent, all of us mulling over Eike's story and what this means for Stronghold Inc. Douglass is housing a wanted man and a dead man. Greyson will come for both of us. And he won't stop until he has our heads.

Unless...

"I came to get evidence against Greyson," I say. "We can stop him from hurting anyone else if you help me out."

Eike smiles. "I've already got what you need."

I frown. "What do you mean?"

He pulls a flash drive from his pocket and sets it on Douglass's desk. "Video footage from Greyson Gem's warehouse. He had the security tapes wiped so there would be no evidence to show police when he reported you for breaking into the place. I got a copy of the tapes before they were scrubbed."

That's the footage of me being tied up, beaten, and shot. It's not what I was looking for—I'd wanted to dig up evidence about Grey and his father throwing me in prison six years ago. I wanted evidence that he'd hired people to attack Brianna. But this isn't bad intel. It's his own warehouse surveillance, undeniable testimony that'll show Greyson giving the order for his men to pound me. Greyson pulling out his gun. Greyson pulling the trigger. Everything we need to nail him.

But it'll also show Eike standing there and watching. An accessory to the crime.

One look at Eike's face and I know he's thought about this already. It's probably the reason he hasn't turned the flash drive in yet. That, and the fact that we have to be careful. With

Greyson's uncle being Police Commissioner, and clearly on Greyson's side, we can't be too sure that things will go our way if we go to the cops.

"Turn it in," Eike says quietly. He's staring at the floor as he speaks. "I know I'm on the tape. But I also know that Greyson Gem needs to pay for what he did." He looks as me now, his grey eyes somehow burning with fire. Like the smoldering grey of a hot, ashen ember.

"You're one of us, Rob. Greyson needs to pay for touching a Stronghold guard."

"Think about what this means for you," Douglass urges. His voice is low, so deep that it's barely more than a rumble in his chest. It fills the room and swells around us, like a warning that lingers even after he's spoken.

"I've thought about it," Eike assures us. "I'm not afraid of going to jail."

He should be. Only guys who've never been to jail aren't afraid of it—because they don't know what it's like. They don't know what to fear. But I've been there, and I'd never wish that experience on my own worst enemy. Except Greyson, of course.

But not Eike. He stood there and watched me almost die, but I know he's sorry. I know he would have helped if he thought he wouldn't get killed in the process. He doesn't deserve to rot in prison for that.

I reach for the flash drive and pass it back to Eike. "You turn it in."

His eyes stretch, making them bulge a little. "Why me?

You're the victim here."

My boss catches on. "You'll be able to make a deal with prosecution if you hold the evidence." He nods approvingly, and I can see the gears turning in his head, a plan forming. "I'll call a lawyer and make arrangements so you can walk into the police station with a plan. In the meantime, make copies of that footage. We'll release it to the public if law enforcement tries to screw us over."

"Public outrage will force them to arrest Greyson for this," I say.

Douglass nods. "But we only release the video if we must. First, we'll try to do things the right way."

"Thank you," Eike says, squeezing the drive in his palm.

"Thank God," I correct him.

23

Bobby assures me the choice is mine when he comes to my apartment with a copy of the security footage. He says Eike is prepared to go to the police with a lawyer, but we should be ready to release the video ourselves in case we're dealing with dirty cops.

"But we don't have to," he says as he slides the flash drive across the kitchen counter to me. "Greyson hasn't made any moves. He might be running scared since he knows I'm alive. There's a chance he'll leave us alone. We could just let this go. Put it behind us and move on."

I shake my head. It's a tempting offer, but there's no way Greyson will truly let this go. Even if its ten years from now, he'll come for my store again. And he'll come for Bobby. And when he does, he'll make sure he doesn't fail again.

I take the drive and squeeze it. It's a little piece of plastic, but it holds my brother's fate. And so much more.

"Think about your family," Bobby murmurs, sliding his arm around my shoulders.

I've never had a great relationship with my parents. My father was always disappointed, and my mother was always displeased. But this is different. Greyson will lose his stores and go to prison if I agree to let Eike turn in the evidence. Whatever hope I had at ever making peace with my parents will go up in flames if I agree to do this. I haven't spoken to my mother or father in weeks—they've been icy since I asked my mom and her church friends to leave my apartment that evening with Verna.

Still… I don't want to lose them completely. And I don't want sweet Verna to suffer either. She's not just my cousin, she's the daughter of the Police Commissioner. This evidence won't prove that Greyson played a part in having Bobby wrongfully convicted six years ago, but it could open the doorway for an investigation if we push hard enough.

Once we go down that road, it's inevitable that my father and uncle will be exposed. Verna will be shamed and dragged through the media as the Commissioner's daughter. I've been in the hot seat before. I know what it's like to have people who don't even know you hate everything about you.

I faced that sort of judgment from my own hometown church. It's a brutal sort of pain, not like being stabbed in the back, more like a blunt punch to the gut. The air rushing out of your lungs, your eyes watering. It's a pain you never forget, a lingering ache that never goes away.

It's that ache, that reminder of all the struggles I faced when I got ostracized from my own church, that makes me pause. What will the congregation think of Verna if everything falls apart? They'll call her the daughter of a liar. Probably say she's a liar too, a wolf in sheep's clothing.

Or maybe they won't... Maybe I was a unique case. Unliked because I was honestly rebellious, not because I was innocent and undeserving of such scrutiny.

I shake my head. I don't want to think about this right now. But I've got to make a decision.

Bobby squeezes me, his hand so large that his fingers curl around my whole arm, almost touching at the fingertips. There isn't a ring on his finger yet, we've had no time to talk about the engagement, but I can't keep my mind from drifting in that direction.

There's more at stake here than my relationship with my parents or Verna's reputation. My future is on the line. Bobby's future is on the line. And beyond that, I feel like it's our responsibility to do the right thing.

God saved Bobby's life that night. He intervened when He didn't have to, saving Bobby and sparing me of the misery that would've followed in the wake of his death. I can always repair my relationship with my parents. It'll take time, but it can happen through prayer and fasting. Verna is strong. She helped me through the worst years of my life. I'm strong enough to help her through hers.

And Greyson deserves to stand trial for the crimes he's committed.

Colonel Gem isn't innocent either. Neither is my Uncle Lee. But their time will come too, and even if I don't have the power to make sure they don't get away with their corruption,

I know they will face a God who righteously judges sin. One day, their wrongs will be righted. For now, I'm fine with this.

"This is the first step," I whisper to Bobby.

He surprises me by shaking his head. "The first step is forgiving them."

I sigh. Greyson's done so much evil. My father's never been kind. And I can't believe my uncle ever played a part in any of this. But the evidence is there, and Bobby's story is real.

Have I forgiven them?

I glance over at Bobby; his crystal blue eyes are filled with concern. Two pools of emotion threatening to overflow.

"It's hard," I say quietly.

He pulls me against him, the scruff of his facial hair scratches my forehead. It's been a few days since he's shaved. With everything that's happened, I've barely even slept. Poor Lyla's been handling the store alone, I've done what I can from my apartment—Hans has been here around the clock, convinced I won't be safe outside until Greyson is behind bars. And Bobby's been bouncing around New York, meeting with his boss and a few lawyers.

"I forgave them." Bobby's voice is a husky whisper.

"You did?" I ask.

I feel him nod. "In the hospital. When I realized there really was a God and that He was kind enough to look past my sins. If He could forgive me, then I have no choice but to forgive others. That's why I'm telling you the decision is yours, Bri. I'm at peace with everything." He sighs. "I want Greyson to go to jail, but not so I can have my vengeance. I want him

248

locked up because he's dangerous and unpredictable."

I nod, tucking my chin down so I can rest my head against Bobby's chest. It's warm in his embrace, wrapped up in his arms like he could protect me from the world. But I'll always be in danger so long as my crazy brother is loose out there.

That has to be my motivation. That has to be my focus. Not vengeance. Not angry payback.

I've got to forgive Greyson, just the same way I forgave Bobby and the same way I must forgive my parents and the church people who hurt me for so long.

Jesus, help me, I pray inside. It's not always easy. It hurts to just let it all go. I feel like I've become addicted to the pain; like it's a part of me now, a hollow pit that's opened inside me, dug out and excavated with the utmost care.

Pain is not a gaping black hole with jagged scars webbing through me. It's a handcrafted tunnel leading straight to my heart.

But that tunnel can be closed off and the emptiness inside me can be filled if I allow it. I can feel the tug inside me, a pull from my center—from my *soul*. It's a Still Voice telling me that I am loved. That I am precious. And that there is nothing to fear about letting go. About forgiving and moving on.

I slowly nod my head. "I can forgive them," I whisper more to myself than to Bobby, but he hears it anyway and responds by kissing the top of my head. "But moving on may take a little longer than it did for you," I admit.

Bobby laughs. "That's okay, Bri. You're not in this alone anymore."

My heart flutters. Bobby is right here with me, and he doesn't care what decision I make. He'll support me no matter what.

"I've got you, Bri," he says, kissing my head again. It's such a simple gesture, probably the most chaste kiss he's ever given me. But it means the world right now. It's a kiss that anchors me to this moment, reminds me of the fact that I'm truly not alone and that I never will be again.

Bobby pulls away to gather the dishes from our lunch. We enjoyed canned soup with sandwiches he made. I fiddle with the flash drive while he rinses our bowls.

"Have you seen the video?" he asks in a shy voice.

I shake my head. "I don't want to see it."

It's hard enough trying to forgive and move on, watching Bobby get beaten and shot will start the process over. Stir up that angry thirst for vengeance I had when I first learned the truth. But I don't want vengeance anymore. I want justice.

I stand and slide the drive back across the counter. "Tell Eike he can go to the police tomorrow. I'll be on standby with the video in case things go south."

Bobby dries his hands on a towel and splays them on the counter, staring down at the drive. "Where will you post it?"

"Across social media. I'll probably mail a copy to a few news outlets too."

If my Uncle Lee refuses to press charges against Greyson on his own, we'll force his hand with public outcry.

Bobby nods and moves to stand beside me. He tucks his hands into his pockets, his eyes glued to my face, studying me.

250

"Are you ready for this, Bri?"

"Are you?" I ask.

He chuckles, sending zings of delight through my chest and stomach. "As long as you're with me, I'm ready for anything."

"I'm not going anywhere," I say.

"Neither am I." He pulls me in a for a hug and says it again, like he isn't sure I've heard. "Neither am I."

It's a promise between us, an oath, a vow, a covenant. We were separated for six years—six of the worst years of our lives—but God brought us back together. He helped us grow and put the worst behind us, so we can enjoy the rest of our years side by side.

No matter what happens, we will never be apart again.

Bobby pulls away and takes my hand. "I'll make the call."

I nod, squeezing his fingers. "Thank you, Bobby. For never forgetting. For being brave enough to come back. Brave enough to love me."

He smiles. "You were brave too. It was tough to come back, but it wasn't easy for you to let me in." He leans down and kisses my cheek. "Now that I'm here, I'm not going anywhere, Princess. I promise."

Epilogue

Three Months Later

The news anchor seems excited as she announces Greyson's trial has finally come to an end. The whole case was pretty straight forward with undeniable video evidence. Still, Greyson's lawyers put up a good fight, claiming there was lost footage of me breaking into the warehouse and that him and his men were just defending his diamonds.

Nobody believed that story.

"Greyson Gem has been sentenced to seven years in prison without the possibility of parole," the news lady says.

Brianna scoots closer to me on the sofa, her eyes sharply focused on the television. She's been a trooper throughout the trial, keeping her head up and ignoring the hateful mail we sometimes get. Her parents haven't spoken to her since Grey was taken into custody. Verna's been by the apartment and doesn't seem to be holding any grudges, probably because the Commissioner isn't under any suspicion. Yet.

Eike's lawyer says he wants to push for another

investigation, start asking questions about what happened six years ago. Shine some light on my innocence and reveal the corruption of Colonel Gem and Commissioner Lee.

It could be years before the truth gets out. But I don't care. I've got the woman I love and a God who loves us both. I'm at peace.

The news switches and starts up a report on me as the victim of Greyson's brutal attack. Everyone has been asking the same question—why did it happen? Why did Brianna's older brother kidnap and shoot me?

I've been avoiding the media and Greyson hasn't opened up either. We've all come to the silent conclusion that it's best to leave things as they are. We don't want any more attention than what we've got, letting it slip that Greyson was after his sister's own business wouldn't have helped the case at all. It would have given the news more things to gossip about.

Brianna switches the television off and sinks into the pillows. She doesn't speak for a long moment.

"How are you feeling?" I ask gingerly.

"I'm happy. But also sad."

"You did the right thing."

She nods. "I know. I'm glad it's behind us now."

"Let's get ready for work," I say, rising from the sofa. There have been crowds gathered outside the store since Greyson was first arrested. It's helped the business, honestly, but it's made my job crazy difficult, and it's been stressing Brianna out.

She hired another assistant to open the store so Lyla can

sneak in an hour later once the crowd has gotten bored, and then we can sneak in during lunchtime when they've gone to grab food. It leaves us the morning to lounge around and enjoy each other, but I can tell Bri's getting tired of the hassle.

She groans at the mention of work and lifts her hands to massage her temples. The sunlight winks off her wedding ring.

We got married two months ago after having a *very* short engagement. I'm a new Christian so the whole wait-until-marriage thing was very painful and very unbearable for me. We decided it was best to just get married instead of testing the limits of our self-control.

The ceremony was small, Lyla, Hans, and me and Bri downtown at the Justice of Peace. We went bowling afterward, Brianna got a perfect score, and then we came back to the apartment, and I made desperate love to my wife like she was the last woman on Earth.

Our days have been spent together, almost every second of every minute. I'm still working as her security—on an extended contract as her personal guard. Brianna jokes that she's never going to release me, so she'll always be my one client. I don't mind at all. The contract is good pay, and I've got a ridiculously expensive wedding ring to pay off. I bought it   from Bri's store, but it was a surprise so I didn't get a discount. Lyla refused to pass me one, saying Brianna would notice the price change in the system and question her about it.

Oh well, it gave me the chance to truly surprise her with the ring. And it gives me joy knowing it's the first really nice thing I've ever bought for her—that and the therapy we've been going to.

It was Brianna's idea for us to take couples counseling at an office her cousin recommended, *Crown Clinic*. I said I would cough up the money for it since Bri's paying for our apartment and our bills and, like, everything else. I know my wife's a millionaire, but I'm still a man. I still want to take care of her however I can. I still want to pay for whatever I can, which includes these weekly sessions together.

We went through a lot these past few months. It was exciting to be reunited with the woman I love, and even more exciting to have her love me in turn, but we can't overlook what we experienced along the way.

Brianna was assaulted multiple times. I was kidnapped and almost murdered. God saved us, brought us back to Him and in Him we found each other. But we haven't been left without scars.

Bri has nightmares sometimes, dreams of that masked man who slashed her up before I came back to town. And sometimes I swear I can feel someone watching me, like— somehow—Greyson's not really in custody. Like he found a way to rig the system in his favor yet again, that he's actually lurking right around the corner. Waiting to whack me over the head and finish what he failed to do three months ago.

It's behind us now. It's all over. But sometimes the enemy likes to attack you afterward, just to spoil your victory celebration.

The fact that Greyson only got seven years makes me

nervous. Makes me wonder if there will be problems in the future. By the time he gets out, Bri and I will have kids of our own. More people to protect. But I can't focus on the what ifs. I won't live the new life God has given me glancing over my shoulder back into the past. I'm going to trust that He's still on the throne. Still in control of everything. I'm going to have faith that He'll keep us safe.

I fought my battles on my own before and it nearly got me killed. I learned the hard way that trusting God isn't always easy, but it is worth it in the end.

Crown Clinic has been helping Brianna and I cope with everything, not just as individuals, but as a couple. Together. They've helped us understand that we can take these nightmares and fears to Christ Jesus. Have them washed away in His blood. It hasn't been easy but, little by little, I'm learning it is possible. I'm learning that there's been more good than bad.

Brianna's store is doing so much better, all the reporters outside have been like free advertisement. Even Jäger Diamonds has been struggling to match our pace. We picked out a set of diamonds for our upcoming Christmas display and put a wonderful down payment on the pretty rocks. Brianna even makes enough to hire Hans three days a week now—he keeps watch over Lyla and the new assistant when I'm not in.

Bri's parents are still icy toward her, but it feels more like a cold chill rather than the frozen, subzero storm from before. They hate that Brianna turned Grey in, but even they couldn't ignore that he was a monster. And that he'd been dead wrong in trying to have me killed. Even though I hate how little time Grey got for kidnapping and attempted murder, part of me is glad for the sake of Bri's parents.

It doesn't feel very great, knowing Greyson will be out on the streets again in less than ten years. I know good ol' Commissioner Lee had something to do with his light sentence. But if Greyson had gotten locked up for life, I'm afraid Brianna's parents never would have forgiven her. There would be no chance for reconciliation.

In a sad way, Greyson's slap on the wrist is a good thing for the family. A good chance at one day living a normal, happy life altogether. Maybe it's just hopeful thinking, but hope was all I had for a long time and look what it's brought me. Add that to my newfound faith and I feel like anything is possible.

Best of all, I have the woman of my dreams now and I have a Father who loves me infinitely more than she ever could. So even if everything else had fallen apart, I'd still be happy. Because I've got Brianna. Because I've got God.

I'm not alone anymore, and I never will be again.

I take Bri's hand and give it a kiss. "You won't have to face the crowds alone."

She smiles. "I know."

"I'm right here, babe."

She doesn't reply, but I don't need her to. Brianna knows how much I love her. She knows that I'm always going to be here. Not just because she hired me, or even because I married her. I'm here because it's where I want to be. Forever.

Enjoy the original trilogy...

Withered Rose

Rosa De Luca is a Christian woman kidnapped and forced to marry a mafia boss. How does she manage to steal his heart? More importantly, how does she introduce him to God? Enjoy Rosa and Amory's story today!

The Woof Pack

Who is Vito Gerardo? Does he become the mafia monster Brandon trained him to be, or is there hope for his future like Bobby believes? Check out TRC's newest romantic suspense trilogy today!

More books by Valicity Elaine & TRC Publishing!

Christian Fantasy
Cross Academy series
The End of the World series
The Scribe

Christian Science Fiction
I AM MAN series

Christian Romance
The Living Water

Christian Children's Fiction
Too Young

ACKNOWLEDGEMENTS

Thank you so much for making it to the end! I hope you enjoyed reading this story as much as I enjoyed writing it. Please take the time to sign up for my newsletter; you'll stay updated on new releases, sales, and get access to dozens of free Christian books ready for you to download today!

See you soon.

The Rebel Christian Publishing

We are an independent Christian publishing company focused on fantasy, science fiction, and romantic reads. Visit therebelchristian.com to check out our books or click the titles below!

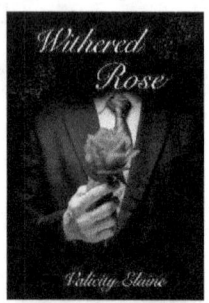

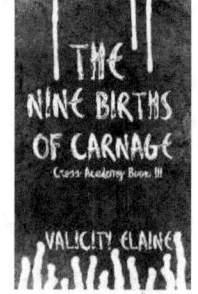

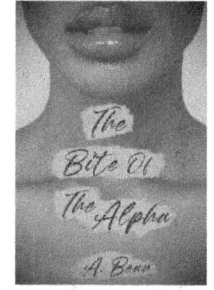

THE END OF THE WORLD

A. BEAN

THE NEW WORLD ORDER

A. BEAN

SAVING THE WORLD

A. BEAN

I AM MAN

Valicity Elaine

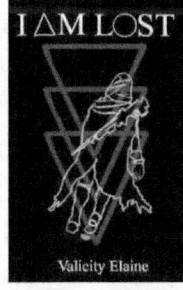

I AM LOST

Valicity Elaine

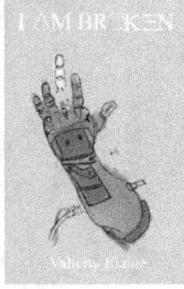

I AM BROKEN

Valicity Elaine

I AM FREE

Valicity Elaine

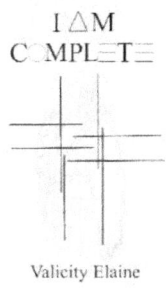

I AM COMPLETE

Valicity Elaine

The Scribe

A. Bean

THE LIVING WATER

A. BEAN

Fractured Diamond

Valicity Elaine

PATCHES

Valicity Elaine

The I Word

Valicity Elaine

www.ingramcontent.com/pod-product-compliance
Lightning Source LLC
Chambersburg PA
CBHW071852220626
47052CB00002B/79